WHAT IS

A Word not only for the South Africa of today but also for the Body of Christ.

Published by : **OUT OF AFRICA PUBLISHERS**
P.O. Box 34685
KANSAS CITY, MO 64116
U.S.A.
(816) 452-5315

Printed in the United States of America

ISBN: 1-888529-03-2

TABLE OF CONTENTS

1.	ANOINTED FOR CHANGE	5
2.	VISION	12
3.	STAY YOUR GROUND	19
4.	ANOINTED TO SERVE	25
5.	THE NATIONS AWAIT!	31
6.	REVIVAL	37
7.	IF MY PEOPLE.....	45
8.	EXPORTED RELIGION	53
9.	THE SOCIAL GOSPEL	59
10.	CRY FOR HELP	65
11.	MISSIONS	73
12.	TRANSITION	78

CHAPTER ONE

ANOINTED FOR CHANGE

During times of great crisis, men will be either cast more upon God or propelled away from Him. Every crisis is a new beginning: new opportunities, challenges and directions are present for which there is a need to rise to the occasion. For some, however, crisis means only death and death is the inability to bend and adapt to a new situation. The strength in the Royal Palm to survive the most formidable storms is because it will bend in the gale force winds. During Hurricane Andrew which hit Florida in 1992 causing over $14 billion in damage with up to 180 miles per hour winds, not a single engineering feat of man could withstand such a storm. And yet, the ingenious design of our Almighty God showed the simple yet elegant Royal Palm bending 360° in the midst of the tempest without being destroyed. Some of the palm fronds may have been shredded but the trees themselves survived.

South Africa is in a major crisis: crisis of direction, identity, trust and nationhood. Many people have already thrown up their hands in horror and given up any fight or will to survive in the land. Many have left in despair while others are ready to flee at a moment's notice. There are those who have adopted the stand of, "Kay Serah, Serah, whatever will be, will be...." Such fatalistic approaches point to some major flaws in the society, namely that South Africans for the most part do not believe in the ability of an awesome God to intervene in their affairs as a whole, or that for the individual, He cannot undertake. Such evaluations are totally erroneous. Recently while I was buying a battery for my watch in a jeweller's shop in Pretoria the assistant began to ask what I thought of the current South African situation. I explained that Jesus didn't really care what happened but that He was more concerned about her personal life. She went on to say after some discussions, that a Portuguese South African had told her, *"I think God is angry with this country....."* That may well be a very true observation supported by many Biblical examples of God's displeasure with peoples and nations because of their sins or their unwillingness to do what He had commanded. Jonah ended in the belly of a whale, Saul lost a Kingdom, while the entire nation of Israel went into Babylonian captivity.

The church in South Africa has failed to give purpose and direction to a nation in crisis. In 1985 there was a mighty move of God in response to prayer and fasting but that is over a decade ago. Where are the national days of fasting and prayer? Where are the untied city-wide marches by all believers of all denominations and colours proclaiming Jesus to be Lord? It should be a total affront to all Christians to see the world using the Spirit *"Dove"* symbol with a proclamation of *"PEACE."* Does the South African Church no longer believe that anything is possible with God? Paul the Apostle says, *"For we wrestle not against flesh and blood...."* (Eph 6:12) I am a firm believer in warfare, having seen it effectively operate across the nations of the world and especially in Rhodesia during her war years, yet I see very little spiritual warfare taking place in South Africa. Throughout the Rhodesian war right up until the elections brought the communists to power and beyond, the Rhodesian church was praying, fasting and vigorously involved in spiritual warfare. It is for this reason and this reason alone that Zimbabwe has not degenerated into that typically African dictatorship that has plagued the rest of the continent. There is absolutely no doubt that after the publication of their communist manifesto the hand of God said *"thus far and no further!"* to Robert Mugabe and his gang. Time and again throughout history, men have been pawns in the hand of God who will ultimately bring His purposes to pass. The dictum used by God is adequately summed up by Mordecai to Esther that, *"you have been brought to the Kingdom for such a time as this"* (Est 4:14), viz the deliverance of the Jews but, *"If you do not, deliverance will arise from another source but you and your household shall be cut off."* What powerful words echoing down the annals of time and applicable to all people of all ages. God gives men a supreme opportunity to be His instruments but if they will not arise to the occasion, He will find others who will fulfil His will and plan. But, there is a supreme and eternal price to pay for failure just as there are supreme and eternal rewards for obedience.

South Africa's wrestlings have been much like those of Jacob. When he was finally left alone there wrestled with Jacob none other than the Lord. This wrestling was to take away his old nature: the supplanter, deceiver, double-dealer: the one who over twenty years previously had a Divine Call and proclaimed, *"This is none other than the house of God and the gate of Heaven."* (Gen 28:17). Having had such a divine visitation Jacob then fled His calling and responsibilities because he was comfortable and secure in his deceitful ways. Thank God He never gives up with His people and the nations until their cup of iniquity is full. Then comes judgement.

When Christ saw that He could not prevail over Jacob, the Lord touched and broke his thigh: drastic measures for superior results. God will not hesitate to take drastic measures with His people to obtain His results. I have really had enough of the church blaming the devil for every adverse thing that happens. Often in our stubborn resistance, it might well be the Lord Himself breaking our thigh to change our nature. Only after Jacob's hip was out and shrivelled did he let go and lo and behold, when he finally let go he suddenly had power. Jacob in that moment of breaking was transformed and renewed and only then could *he* take-a-hold of the Lord and declare *"[now] I will not let Thee go except Thou bless me."* (Gen 32:26). The transformed Jacob fought for anointing, for calling, for all that God purposed for him but it was now on God's terms. The blessing finally came when Jesus pronounced him "Israel: Prince with God."

South Africa has been like a Jacob and stands at the crossing of the river Peniel. The wrestling that has taken place has been in flesh and blood just as Jacob initially wrestled with the Lord in his flesh and blood or his carnality. God is not concerned with kingdoms and positions in this world. Jacob had been greedy and was driven to seize by force the birthright and blessing. The only kingdom God is ultimately concerned with is the kingdom within.

Shortly before Pentecost the disciples had asked, *"Lord, when will you restore again the Kingdom of Israel?"* (Acts 1:6). Though it was slowly dawning on this motley band of men that Jesus had come to save us from sin, still they were more concerned with His appearing as the mighty warrior who would drive out the Romans and re-establish David's glorious kingdom in the natural. Jesus offered something far more glorious than the natural restoration of Israel: He offered them a power beyond any man's wildest dreams or imaginations and He offered them the entire earth as their kingdom. Their transformation was going to come through a yieldedness to the Holy Spirit so that the fullness of Christ would fill each one and they would become **LIVING EPISTLES** of His life and glory to the ends of the earth.

That is exactly what the Lord is offering every believer in South Africa. The Holy Spirit is anointing for change in this hour so that God's people in the land might be a witness to the ends of the earth. God is not concerned with territory except for the sake of souls and will bring about His purposes in whatever ways He deems necessary. He used a Nebuchadnezzar to humble Judah and manifest His glory to the Babylonian Empire and then raised up a Cyrus to send Israel home again.

Paul emphasises that the Kingdom is *"not meat and drink but righteousness, peace and joy in the Holy Ghost."* (Rom 14:17). Unfortunately the church has been seduced and deceived by the preaching of other "gospels" which have robbed her of the power and authority given at Pentecost. South Africa is on the threshold of what can be its greatest hour and destiny. The future does not depend on politics or Pretoria, Johannesburg or Cape Town. The future depends on the Church taking her rightful stand and wrestling not in flesh and blood for natural kingdoms but in the spirit against principalities and powers.

White South Africans have become a people of **LAAGER MENTALITY.** While they have remained within the circle determined to hold on to their territory, traditions and life-styles, South Africans of other colours encircled the **"Laager"** threatening war and destruction while all the time grabbing for the same territory and life-style. Sadly, the Church has become embroiled and in the process lost her unique identity, power and integrity as vested by the Lord so as to be a light to the nations.

The issue plaguing this nation may be summed up from opposite sides of the fence. There are those who are worried, "Will I still have my swimming pool, my home in Houghton and my Mercedes Benz?" while at the opposite spectrum are those aspiring and demanding their swimming pool, their home in Houghton and their Mercedes Benz. The problem is that there is just not enough to go around and there never will be. But I want to tell you that God doesn't care about those issues. He cares whether we are changing from glory to glory to be more like His Son. He cares whether we love Him more than we love this present evil world. He cares whether we carry His heart beat for the lost and are doing something about it AND there is enough of Him to go around!

The church has been brainwashed by the "Prosperity Gospel." When 3 John 2 declares, *"....that thou mayest prosper...."* John is not talking of material or financial blessing. "Prosperity" means to be making significant progress in our growth and walk," so much so that the world takes note. It is your life and mine which *"is a city set on a hill and cannot be hid."* (Matt 5:14). The Lord never purposed His people to be walled and fenced because, *"He is our shield and exceeding great reward."* He becomes our defence when we pull down the barriers. open the gates, lift up the doors and become vulnerable. The believer is indeed, the temple city whose builder and maker is God but we have substituted such a glorious heritage for temporal kingdoms and cities all of which will pass away. The world must see and know that God's people have a greater purpose and calling to life than our pools, houses and cars and maintaining the status quo. Jesus was not concerned about the disciples wanting a restoration of old national kingdoms but of His living reality and dynamic within them which would make them so transformed that their very appearance and life would cause men to wonder and cry out, "What must we do to be saved?"

God is delivering South Africans from all the encumbrances of the past. Coloured South African peoples cry about the evils of apartheid but the white South Africans have as much been enslaved and shackled by the same system. Believe me, the blessing and freedom of the peace of which white South Africans have been robbed far outweighs the material prosperity and blessings of positions that apartheid offered to those very same South Africans. The price to pay for not fulfilling God's call is an awesome one. Material blessings can never substitute for the blessings of God. Men who are deprived of the presence and anointing of the Spirit degenerate into animals. A nation which loses God's approval or disobeys His *raison d'etre* degenerates into idolatry and the worst excesses of the flesh. Coloured Christians must be set free from the, *"cursed," "suppressed," "denied"* mentality that has robbed them of their power, dignity and anointing while white Christians need to be released from prejudices and the **Laager** mentality that has robbed them of their high calling.

It was under the harshest persecution of Nero's Rome that the church grew, blossomed and matured. If there's any message to which the Church needs desperately to turn, it is the message of the Cross: suffering and dying to self and rising to the Lordship of Jesus. The moment any believer rejects the "suffering gospel" He negates the power of a resurrected life. Just as long as we hold on to our lives we shall lose them. I well remember a prominent engineer friend of mine who left behind everything he owned in Mocambique during the terrible persecution of the early FRELIMO days. He smuggled out his wife and himself but told of an equally prominent banker friend of his whose wife would not let go. That couple were ready to flee but the wife had to return for her jewels. She snatched her diamonds, pearls, rubies from her dresser but as she rushed down the hall of their palatial home, the FRELIMO soldiers burst in at the front door and shot her dead. Her grief-stricken husband fled alone. Lot's wife was of the same nature: she could not leave Sodom behind and became a pillar of salt as testimony.

The Holy Spirit is anointing every South African for change if one will hear the Spirit's call. He will remove hurts, prejudices, fears, doubts, lusts and take away the desire to hold on desperately to all for which one has worked, laboured, suffered. If one can let go, God will multiply back and there is a glorious mandate awaiting to be fulfilled for South Africa as a nation. People of all colours and cultures can rise up and be a part of what God has for South Africans in this new era.

CHAPTER TWO

VISION

Intercession is not prayer meetings or some intensified form of prayer but of knowing the burden of the heart of God and then living out that burden until a victory has been won with God over the matter of that burden. Prayer can be a very "hit and miss" endeavour but once an intercessor breaks through with God and gains the place of intercession, then the intercessor knows that his cries are fulfilled and will be answered in God's time. Intercession carries with it absolute assurance of answers because interceding the burden of God's heart is interceding His will. Jesus said, *"Ask whatsoever ye will in my name...."* (Jn 15:16). He most certainly was not giving his people licence but when we ask large the burden of God's heart He must, by His very nature, answer.

And so it was during years of intercession that the Lord gave a startling revelation one night. Where there is true spiritual unity consensus must emerge. If the Holy Spirit is speaking and sharing the burden of God's heart He will never give one person a direction without confirming it to and by the majority. He does not tell one person one thing and something contrary to another. Where are the prophets in South Africa speaking with the voice and authority of God, giving direction to a stumbling nation? Rise up and speak the oracles!

The Spirit of the Lord swept over the meeting and there was a great travailing for nations. People began to see different nationals and even speak in their tongues. It was quite evident that the Holy Spirit was trying to arrest the attention of the group and focus on something very important. It was then that one and another and then another person had visions of different parts of the human body. Each part however showed various stages of corruption and decay. It was as if one had walked into some diabolic surgery where a maniac Mengler was at work dismembering and operating and leaving the pieces lying about. Blood and decay were everywhere. Suddenly in the strangest fashion the corrupted and decayed members were brought together by an invisible hand into a human body again.

As the vision unfolded that body began to take on the appearance of nations. The head of the body represented Great Britain. The Spirit of the Lord clearly spoke that Britain had lost her God-given direction and calling because she was a nation which was pleasure-loving and desired only comfort and ease. The head was filled with cancer. There were knots and bulges and the eyes were blinded by disease. The brain could no long function. God continued to speak that Britain had been a nerve centre from which He had directed the setting forth of His Word. She had stood against Rome, sent out the greatest missionaries, colonised most of the world, translated and printed the Bible into many languages and stood against the evils of Hitler. But now, sadly, the post-war generations have settled down to a life of comfort, resting upon the works of the past and though called to be the brain and nerve centre, have left the work to others. Today, the gods of Britain have become the soccer ball and beer bottle and a pleasure-loving society that does not want to be disturbed. It is no wonder the British Royal Family is in such a mess; they merely show the state of the whole nation: a nation which has largely rejected God.

In the vision, God clearly stated that Britain had been called to missionize the whole world and that her mandate is not yet over.

The upper chest area of the corrupted body was manifest as Australia which though bronzed and muscular on the outside was filled with parasites and putrefaction underneath. The lungs were collapsing and a horrifying sickness was taking over the whole chest. Today we know that sickness to be AIDS. *"Australia I called," said the Lord, "to preach the Gospel to Asia and the islands. Alas My people have become corrupted with immorality and the false worship of philosophies and New Age."* Indeed, Australia is one of the most homosexual and New Age nations of the world. Blessed with a high calling, Australians and New Zealanders have filled their lives with the fun of sun, sand and surf and left their high calling in God.

The Lord continued that, *"It was no accident that these nations were founded under My direction to fulfil my plan for the world. I called America into being to win South America and the East with the Gospel but alas my people have missed their mark. I even put it into the heart of Japan to call for missionaries but America would not heed their cry...."* Today, there is a vicious war being waged between America and Japan: not a war with guns as in the past, but a war of trade which the Japanese are winning. Indeed, the Japanese may well have lost World War II but they have subsequently won the peace. The Japanese cried for missionaries to swamp Japan with the Word but nobody heeded their cry in the post war era. Despite General McCarthy's appeal Americans were too bitter with the Japanese to go into that nation and reach them for Jesus. Today Japan is really a hardened nation against missionaries and the Gospel. In the face of the greatest odds, the Japanese rose up to fight again and today, like Germany, they can hold the world to economic ransom. Such a tragic testimony is living proof that Christians cannot become emotionally embroiled in the affairs of the world and allow emotions to corrupt our mandate and calling.

South Africa, you are at a similar cross-roads and God is giving you one last chance to fulfil your high calling. God has a great design for the nation which has never yet been fulfilled. Rise up South Africa and take your rightful place in God's plans for the nations.

America was the lower torso of the sickened body. The lower torso was bulging and debauched through gluttony and riotous living.

Peritonitis was eating away at the inner organs and sapping the strength and vigour of a nation which had been planted by God for the purposes of taking the Gospel to the ends of the earth. In actual fact, the lower torso was clearly depicted as that of Elvis Presley, a young man who once had a relationship with the Lord but had drifted away. Many may argue that America has given much for the preaching of the Gospel. When one considers however, that more money is spent on pet food in the United States than the total given to world missions each year by all denominations, then true giving is lean.

The part of the body representing South Africa was the loins and legs portrayed as those of a marathon runner who had dropped from the race because of muscle cramp and fatigue. There was a great cry of the Spirit, *"Whom shall I send and who will go for us?"* and there was no South African to say, *"Here am I Lord, send me!"*

"Indeed," said the Lord, *"I planted South Africa to be a light and testimony to this great continent of Africa known always as the Dark Continent. I ordained you, South Africa to take My Word, My precepts and My name to all of Africa. I planted in your forefathers that pioneering spirit so that they would move ever onwards bearing the Gospel with them. But alas, the nation has been seduced and deceived. I gave you the riches of gold and diamonds and much more to empower you and provision you for the great task of the mission fields of Africa but you settled down to enjoy the fruits of the land for yourselves. Indeed, because I had planted that adventurous spirit within you and you did not use it for My glory and honour you therefore corrupted it. The Isaac I promised and purposed became an Ishmael in your midst and your energies and efforts were established in building your own kingdoms. Your hands turned against the very peoples I had sent you to win while you sat back to enjoy and squander upon your own lusts the riches I had given you.*

You have built great temples in which to worship Me, thinking that you did Me a favour and service but I have said, 'have we not done thus and thus for Thee O Lord, but I say unto you I know you not according to your works,' for I would have obedience and not your sacrifice. You have corrupted My ways in the land. I have weighed you in the balance and found you wanting, South Africa. Buy of Me gold tried in My Fire. Anoint thine eyes with eyesalve that thou mayest see. Evan as the prodigal son came to his senses, come thou to thine, O South Africa and I will visit you with the wind of My Spirit and I will blow upon you and I will touch you and heal your land that as one, you might fulfil the high calling and anointing which I have purposed for you."

For almost two decades now we have carried South Africa in our hearts, travailing and crying out to God that He would raise up His people to fulfil His vision for the land. For, where there is no vision or word established, the people perish and South Africa is perishing.

The feet of the decayed body represented the nation of Kenya. The feet are powered by the legs and these feet were stilted and broken. The Psalmist declares, *"How lovely on the mountain are the feet of him who brings good news,"* and our feet are to be shod with the "Gospel of Peace." Ah, what a contrast to the feet that run to mischief and create strife. God revealed that Kenya and South Africa were to work hand-in-hand to take the Gospel to Africa and yet, for years they have had no relationship except one of distrust. I well remember flying into Nairobi from Israel during the 1980's. On my arrival at Kenyatta Airport the Kenyan Immigration authorities were not prepared to let me into their country simply because I had a South African immigration stamp in my British passport! Only some fast talking and the mercy of the Lord opened the door but with a stern lecture from the Kenyans that, "we don't want you visiting South Africa." I marvel at how the enemy can really use for destruction those things that God has purposed for good when men will allow the flesh to get in the way. Kenya is the only nation in Africa which tasted a small renewal after the Mau Mau uprising of the 1950's and certainly during the Charismatic renewal of the 1980's she was a key nation in Africa for Gospel Conventions. But, like so many in Africa, the best that the continent has raised up have felt a call to the western industrialised nations. Not only is there a Continental "brain drain," but there is also a Continental "spiritual drain."

It is time for hands to be linked across colour barriers, natural frontiers, tribal and regional boundaries so that there is a continental outpouring of the Holy Spirit. I have witnessed the genocide in Zimbabwe where Shona "ethnically cleansed" Matabele. A very good friend of mine, a mighty evangelist during the days of Rhodesia, was a Matabele. Led by the Holy Spirit he chose a Shona to be his bride. The girl's parents were so incensed that they hired a gang to kill the young man the night before his wedding. He had asked me to be his "best man" as we had been very close intercessors. I was so concerned when he did not meet me at the appointed time that I alerted the police. It was one o'clock in the morning, the day of his wedding, when he arrived at my home bloodied and beaten. He had managed to escape the gang but was begging me to go with him to collect his bride-to-be whom he had hidden as she was about to be kidnapped by her parents. I escorted the young lady to my sister's home where she was then able to prepare for her wedding in safety and security. Imagine! All that nonsense simply because the couple were from different tribes.

One of the greatest heartaches I have ever experienced is running a Bible School in Malawi. Dr. Kamuzu Banda who had been president for thirty years had always insisted proudly that there is no regionalism and no tribalism in Malawi. Our first intake of thirty students was more-or-less divided equally between the southern, central and northern regions. The choice had not been intentional. Things went smoothly for a season whilst the novelty of "settling in" at

Bible School still existed but after six months the school divided on tribal lines and from students who were all born-again, Spirit-filled young men and women. Paul experienced similar problems in the early church which led him to emphasise, *"There is neither Jew not Greek, bond nor free, male nor female."* (1 Cor 12:13).

It is time for all believers across all nations to realise that our allegiance is to the flag and anthem of heaven: our Captain is none other than Jesus Christ and that we look for a city whose builder and maker is God. The heavenly Jerusalem. However shall we be the light to the world if we are divided? Jesus said a house divided against itself cannot stand (Matt 12:25). He went on to say that, *"I will build My Church and the gates of hell shall never prevail....."* (Matt 16:18). I see the gates of hell prevailing against much of the "Church" and must therefore conclude that it cannot be the Lord's Church: it must be men's programmes, men's ideas, men's buildings, men's organisations.

Oh beloved, the time is long overdue for we Africans to join hands and work for the salvation of the nations of Africa and the world.

CHAPTER THREE

STAY YOUR GROUND

"There will NOT BE CIVIL WAR in South Africa." I declared this six weeks before the elections and it is still time now. Fighting and strife will continue for a long time but there will not be a civil war. South Africa has been called of God and His hand is upon the nation. He is giving the people of God a last chance to fulfil that High Calling and mandate and He will keep his hand staying the land. Be assured of this.

There is nothing more infuriating and heart-breaking than to see spiritual leaders and their families flee from situations of strife. Either God called His people or He did not. If a person is called, then God is well able to protect and keep those who are His. Let us never forget that it might be in the will of God that people die for their faith. The martyr company is not yet complete and it is true that the "blood of the martyrs is the seed of the church." I was great friends of the Elim missionaries who were butchered to death in their mission school in the Vumba of Eastern Rhodesia in 1978. An incredible volume of prayer ascended for the perpetrators of that massacre. Today, of the group all but two are saved and eighty percent are in full-time ministry, planting churches and establishing the Word of God in the lives of multitudes.

I have lived in many war zones of Africa and often seen that the first peoples to leave when strife brews are the missionaries. What a shame and how hollow we make the Gospel. Christians are continually mocked by Moslems. Why? Because the latter are ready to fight and die for what they believe. Most Moslems think that we have a weak God because we Christians are not ready to die for the faith. We would rather spend our lives running. And, I might re-iterate that Allah is a demon prince and not the Jaweh of Israel or the Lord Jesus Christ who is God.

What kind of shepherd leaves his flock in the midst of the storm? I know many pastors in Rhodesia who, whilst assuring their congregations that they were remaining through thick and thin, were in actual fact making secret trips to South Africa, Australia, Great Britain and the U.S.A. to set up an office or find a church. I have heard that some prominent South African pastors were doing the same: "contingencies you know!" Shame on you. You are nothing but hirelings. If God called you and planted you He will also protect you. I also do not believe that a husband has any right to send out his wife and children. The God who called the man also called the family. If He didn't you shouldn't have been there in the first place. During tremendous political upheavals in Malawi in 1992-93 there was a particular day when the whole city of Blantyre seemed to go berserk. There is no doubt that strong demon powers were stirring up great strife. Many missionaries and Indian traders sent their families out of the country. What a testimony! Anyway, at our mission we had several single women missionaries who had been through some tough battles in Mocambique and Malawi. They were not about to budge! Cars were being overturned and smashed, shops looted, road blocks set up by thugs and general chaos ensued which was the kind of anarchy which causes governments to be overthrown. The ladies were on the opposite side of Blantyre. Using back streets and side roads, I managed to reach them and escort them to a point which I was sure was absolutely safe. Now, to reach our mission headquarters requires travelling through a major township or "high density suburb" as they are known in Malawi. Most white people will not venture through the area including the missionary fraternal. Firstly, we are living on the "wrong side of the tracks," so to speak and secondly it's deemed, "too dangerous."

As I had ventured out on my "rescue mission" that afternoon, I noticed a great number of people massing on the roads but after all, it is a very high density suburb and there are always thousands of people about so I was not unduly concerned.

I sent the lady missionaries on their way with instructions not to stop for anyone but alas, as they turned the corner into the township they came face to face with a solid wall of humanity! "There seemed about 10,000 hostile people on the road ready for blood," the missionaries later declared. "We threw up our hands in horror and cried out, 'Lord, HELP!' There was nothing else to do!"

The people had already looted groceries stores and were a volatile, seething mass of humanity. Suddenly and without explanation the people began to part like a huge wave and made a literal highway for the vehicle. The missionaries drove down this perfect "avenue" flanked on both sides by masses of angry people. They reached the mission in perfect safety while vehicles behind them were smashed.

A week later after calm was restored, our mission children returned to school and were given the following incredible account by the township children.

"When your missionaries came on that day we saw that they were going to be in trouble. You know we do love your missionaries - they always help us, talk to us and play with us. So, when we saw your car we all (the children) shouted, 'leave these people. They are our friends. Let them pass.'"

With that, the adults obeyed not the voice of children but the voice of Almighty God speaking out of the mouths of babes. What an awesome God and what protecting power!

It is time to "know our God" in the midst of the storm. Dan 11:32 says they who KNOW shall be mighty and do exploits. We want to be "exploit-makers" in this hour, the greatest hour of the church. Never have there been such opportunities to do things for the Lord which will echo down the annals of eternity. No task is too great for any believer for we have an unlimited God with unlimited resources.

I am grateful for the great stirrings which take place every now and then for it exposes those who, though they might be eloquent preachers and teachers, are not Calvary material. Let such men move on and clear the way for the new breed which has been stifled by them for too long.

To those who leave deceitfully, God can never and will never prosper them until they return and repent. The many in Rhodesia who left under such conditions have never prospered in their adoptive lands. Those, however, who were honest and asked leave of their congregations to depart, have been blessed. But, there is always a price to pay for fleeing **unless** God clearly commands to "flee from this city," but then it is "unto the next." I highly esteem that noble band of missionary martyrs who set forth from England's shores during the last Century: the Hudson-Taylors to China, Jonathan and Rosalind Goforth to China and Korea, C.T. Studd to the "Heart of Africa," Amy Carmichael to Dohnovur, India and an almost endless list of other Christians giants. Such peoples were not afraid of leaving behind their wealth - and most were affluent - to plunge into the most remote regions of a hostile world and lose their lives that others might live. Oh that that spirit, dedication and sacrifice would pervade the church again. Oh, for a fearless company of Christendom who will not merchandise the Word and anointing, who will not seek the life of comfort and ease, who will be ready to die for our Lord who gave His all for us. Oh may that character of Christ invade us all once again, *"Who being equal with God thought it not robbery... but made Himself of no reputation, took upon Himself the form of {the lowest bond slave who would wash His disciples feet} becoming conformable unto death even the death of {a tree upon which anyone who was hanged was cursed}."* (Phil 2:6-8).

Our confidence is only in the Lord for it is, *"The Spirit which is life - the flesh profits nothing."* (John 6:63). South Africans are a resilient, hard-working people who are always ready to "maak 'n plan."

Dedicated and also aggressive, they have fought for their very existence but know also when to yield. Such character traits make for resourceful missionaries and people who will take the Gospel to the ends of the earth.

It is character which is the pivotal point of good evangelism and missionary work. According to Sherwood Eddy, a missionary statesman and author, "Every normal missionary sails with high purpose but as a very imperfect Christian.... His character is his weakest point...." Time and again I have seen this on the mission field whilst always being conscious of my own character and dealings. God is wanting vessels filled with His glory and power.

I want to return to the issue of the blessed and the called. It is abundantly evident through the promises made by God to Abraham that whoever came out of Abraham's loins would be blessed and multiplied. Now, even although Ishmael was the product of carnal manipulation, he was nevertheless, fruit of Abraham and fell within the terms of the covenant God had established with that patriarch. God had said, *"And I will make thee exceedingly fruitful and I will make nations of thee and kings shall come out of thee...."* (Gen 17:6). Ishmael's descendants were twelve princes and twelve tribes who were supremely blessed (Gen 17:20) but when Abraham grieved for Ishmael the Lord clearly affirmed in the Hebrew emphatic tense, *"For in Isaac shall thy seed be **CALLED**."* (Gen 21:12). Immediately we are presented with the stark reality of Ishmael who was blessed but Isaac who was called. Ishmael was blessed because he was the seed of Abraham and God's gifts and callings are without repentance. But, Ishmael was a persecutor of Isaac and Ishmael's descendants have ever persecuted Israel. Indeed, up to this very hour, Ishmael is blessed. No other part of desert real estate could hold the entire world to ransom as did the Arab nations with oil during the 1980's and it will happen again

The issue of the blessed versus the called is the issue of prosperity versus the anointing and there is a vast difference between them because the anointing carries with it the whole concept of the birthright. The birthright was the belief that from the son who held it would come *the* Son, the Saviour, the Messiah, the Man-Child promised by God to Adam and Eve. Eve mistakenly in her rebellion, supposed that man-child to be Cain saying, *"I have gotten a man-child from the Lord."* (Gen 4:1). Now in Biblical times, whoever had the birthright automatically received with it the greater portion of the inheritance which was also called the "Blessing." The converse was not true however. Thus in the example of Jacob and Esau we see the enormity of Esau's crime in despising his birthright. In so doing, he automatically, in the eyes of God, lost also the blessing. Today the principle is still in operation. Many aim for the blessings and prosperity instead of the anointing.

Now beloved, the anointing has a price tag; a high price tag, for which few people want to pay and it is this anointing which will differentiate between the profane and the Holy, the blessed and the called.

CHAPTER FOUR

ANOINTED TO SERVE

The anointing is not a gift or a blessing which is bestowed by the laying on of hands. The anointing is God's stamp of approval or mark of authority in recognition of our standing and relationship with Him. The holy anointing oil of the Old Testament was made of four very costly spices blended together and a hin of pure olive oil which united them. Gethsemane means "oil press" and it was as a result of Christ's sufferings - a costly pressing out of His very life - that the anointing oil of the Holy Spirit was poured out for the Church, His body.

The word in Hebrew for "Anointed" is "Mashiyach" which speaks of "the anointed one;" a consecrated person: prophet, priest or king who was "set apart" for the purposes of God. In particular it pointed to the Messiah, Christ Jesus, **THE** anointed of God.

The Greek word for "anointed" is "CHRISTOS' from which we get :

1. CHRIO : The Greek verb "to anoint"
2. CHRISTOS : The Greek noun "the anointed"
3. CHRISMA : The Greek noun "the anointing." This is NOT to be confused with the Greek CHARISMA which is gift from which we get Charismata (gifts) and Charismatic. Just because somebody exercises some gifts does not necessarily mean they have the ANOINTING. The "Charismatic" Church has confused this issue.

Now in the Old Testament :

1. The ANOINTER : Usually a Prophet, for example, Samuel
2. The ANOINTED : Usually a King, Prophet or Priest, for example, David.
3. The ANOINTING: Holy Anointing Oil made according to God's specific instructions.

In the New Testament pertaining to the Godhead :

1. The ANOINTER :God, the Father
2. The ANOINTED : Jesus Christ the Son
3. The ANOINTING: The Holy Spirit (Dove at the Baptism)

In the New Testament pertaining to the church :

1. The ANOINTER : Father and the Son
2. The ANOINTED : The Body, the Church, the Believer.
3. The ANOINTING: The Holy Spirit

The reason for such an explanation is that, in accordance with the TRIUNE PATTERN the three offices of the Old Testament namely Prophet, Priest and King are still operational in this dispensation of grace under the Anointer who gives the Anointing (Holy Spirit) to the Body. In the New Testament then:

1. Prophetic Anointing

This is speaking forth the Anointed Word. It does not apply to prophets only but all who are servants of God. It is the Word of power "dunamos" which is set forth to achieve a purpose and does so.

2. **Priestly Anointing**
(We are *all* believer priests after the order of Christ Jesus) is the Ministry of Reconciliation which incorporates prayer, praise, worship and intercession. How necessary it is for this anointing to be operating in South Africa in these days.
3. **Kingly Anointing**
(He has made us Kings and Priests) which is the operation of the Government of God in ruling, reigning, authority and power, NOT in the natural, but over all the works of the enemy.

It is simply imperative that we distinguish between the natural and the spiritual. It is time that every believer stepped out in boldness to operate in the prophetic, priestly and kingly anointing. All three you may ask? Indeed, most certainly. It has become the privilege of every believer to walk in all three anointings, whereas in actuality most believers seldom flow in a single anointing. If individuals can be anointed, so then can whole nations.

Whenever we speak it should be under the prophetic anointing, sending forth God's Word with power and authority to achieve its intended purpose. The main reason that there is no prophetic anointing is because there is no priestly anointing. Our outward lives and ministry should be a direct expression of our private devotions with the Lord.

The corporate anointing in a fellowship is the sum of the individual anointings. People's attitude to, and their flow in worship and intercession, will immediately determine the level of anointing. It is like a spiritual barometer. And, it is in private devotions - alone in the closet - where we gain the Lord's stamp of approval.

The Spirit of the Lord continually transverses the earth seeking out those whose hearts are inclined towards Him. The Spirit will always come to rest where the anointed word or prophetic word is operating and that will be where the priestly anointing flows. The Spirit and the Word bring forth life. In Genesis the Spirit moved upon the face of the waters. When God spoke, Creation came into existence. In the same fashion, Noah sent out the dove, a symbol of the Holy Spirit which brought back life in the form of the olive stem. David, sitting attending sheep on the hillsides around Bethlehem, had learned to flow in that priestly ministry. He thereby received God's stamp of approval which was confirmed when Samuel arrived and anointed him to be the future King of Israel. The fact must be emphasised that David had already been sealed by the Holy Spirit for that service because of his priestly ministry before the Lord in prayers, praises, worship and intercessions. The priest ministers unto the Lord and then, coming out of the sanctuary, ministers unto the people in the prophetic anointing.

The weakness of the church is that there are too few priests: men who can stand boldly in the presence of God because of the price they have paid. It is the Priestly Anointing that also gives the Kingly authority. I am greatly disturbed at the lack of intercession and spiritual warfare in the church. It is time that believers accepted that they can influence the outcome of events by binding the forces and principalities of darkness. I am quite horrified that in the new Constitution, South Africa is not boldly declared as a Christian country. Instead, people are free to believe whatever they want. This therefore, legitimises witchcraft and satanism. There is no stand against homosexuality and immorality and the whole fibre of the Bill of Rights and new Constitution shows that there was very little warfare by believers. Psalm 149:6-9 expressly declares that every believer who has the high praises in his mouth - the high praises are a new song - has a two-edged sword in his hand, *"To execute vengeance upon the heathen and punishments upon the people and to bind their kings with chains and their nobles with fetters of iron; to execute upon them the judgement written...."*

Beloved, I have had enough of the nonsense, "Don't judge me...." When Paul declares, *"Judge not lest ye be judged,"* the Greek word is "KRITICOS" from which we get "critical." There is a big difference between having a spirit of criticism and making value judgements. We are called, at all times, to make judgement in the Kingdom but Jesus said: *"Judge righteous judgement."* It is, *"Out of the abundance of the heart the mouth speaketh."* That's judgement! *"By their fruits ye shall know them,"* is a value judgement and so on in the Kingdom. Thus, judgement is already written upon the devil and his angels and all of humanity who line up with his wicked deeds. It is the business of the church to wrestle against such principalities and powers, bind them and pull down their strongholds. This is the Kingly anointing in operation and it is judgmental.

If the South African church would rise up, become militant and possess the land - not the physical kingdom - then there would be changes in the natural. The physical rulers of South Africa would have to change and submit to the Lordship of Jesus whether they like it or not. The Church in South Africa has a few years left to cause the nation to line up with God and His Word and to bind and pull down the strongholds of the ruling principalities. Remember that the government is upon His shoulders. The Ark of the Covenant which was to be carried on the shoulders of the **PRIESTS** represented the glory, presence, throne and government of God on the earth. That authority is vested only in the hands of believers who have the high praises.

It is no wonder there is so much township violence: the ancient princes which have ruled in the atmosphere have not been bound. There were so many testimonies which came out of the Rhodesian war of miraculous interventions and deliverances of God's people for the simple reason that principalities were bound and the enemy could not fulfil his wicked designs.

Oh, that believers of all races and denominations would take hands across South Africa lifting up the banner of Jesus and pulling down the strongholds of the enemy. Oh, that there would be a vision for the evangelism of the land and the whole Continent of Africa. Oh, that the *"Violent"* would press in and take the Kingdom by force

(Matt11:12) and that God's people would get into the sanctuary and obtain that priestly anointing before trying to exercise the prophetic and kingly anointings in the world and before men. The Church is often ridiculed by the world because we go off like a damp squib as it were - instead of like volumes of T.N.T. Why? Because the Church attempts to do and accomplish things without the full authority and approval of God. From where does that come? The inner sanctuary.

CHAPTER FIVE

THE NATIONS AWAIT!

God has always concerned Himself with the nations. In Acts 15:14-17, His purpose is clearly revealed through James when he declares, *"Simeon hath declared how God at the first did visit the Gentiles to take out of them a people for His Name. And to this agree the words of the prophets; as it is written after this I will return and will build again the Tabernacle of David.... THAT THE RESIDUE OF MEN MIGHT SEEK AFTER THE LORD, AND ALL THE GENTILES UPON WHOM MY NAME IS CALLED."*

God called Abraham and promised to make of him a nation. What kind of nation, you may ask? A nation of worshippers who would be a testimony to all peoples. Israel reached the apex of her testimony as a worshipping nations under the reign of King Solomon when all nations came up to Jerusalem to see the splendour, wealth and majesty of the Temple and of Solomon's palaces and kingdom. The testimony of Sheba was that the *"half had not been told,"* and there was no spirit left in that queen who was formidable in her own right.

Now Peter, in his epistle declares that, *"Ye are a chosen generation, a royal priesthood, an holy nation, a peculiar people; that ye should shew forth the PRAISES of Him who hath called you out of darkness into His marvellous light."* (1Pet 2:9). John in Revelation sees a vast sea of believers from every nation, kindred, tongue and tribe WORSHIPPING around the throne (Rev. 5:9-10), while Habakkuk sees a vision of the knowledge of the glory of the Lord filling the whole earth (Hab 2:14). The fullness of God's blessings to Abraham was the multitudes in Abraham's bosom or paradise and that we are all descendants of Abraham by faith. Indeed, his seed is as the sand of the sea (Gen 22:17).

What a formidable testimony South Africa can make in the family of nations but may it be because the glory of the Lord fills the nations and not because of Bafana Bafana, rugby, cricket, apartheid, diamonds or gold. God makes the incredible promise, *"Ask of Me and I will give THE NATIONS as an inheritance and the ends of the earth as a possession."* (Ps :8). The nations of Africa are perishing from sickness, diseases, civil wars and famines. Do you realise that up to 80% of the nation of Uganda is perishing with AIDS? South Africans have been largely isolated from the rest of Africa through politics and are therefore somewhat ignorant of what is happening in the continent. AIDS in Kenya, Tanzania, Malawi, runs from 40-60% and by the close of a decade almost half of the continent will be annihilated by the curse of AIDS. Consider this fact: for the past twelve years there have been up to 1.5 million refugees living in Malawi. Some of the refugee camps have exceeded 200,000 people in a single camp. Imagine the logistics of such undertakings. I have stayed and preached in those camps for weeks on end and seen the conditions. With such a huge static population with little to do the people turn to mischief. Now the refugees are returning home with all the sexually transmitted diseases to further spread them through population groups. Praise God for those who heard and believed the Word and are returning with life in Christ Jesus.

Multitudes upon multitudes of Africa's four hundred and fifty million have never heard the Gospel. During the Mocambican war, we walked thousands of miles in the war zones preaching to and teaching all manner of peoples. Right on South Africa's doorstep is a nation ravaged by over thirty years of continuous war. Do you realise that there are children who were born in war, grew up in war and went to war? A whole generation knows nothing but mines, MiGs, AK47 rifles and torture and death. How well I remember reaching remote villages only to find children fleeing in terror because they'd never seen a white face let alone heard the glorious Gospel. At night the children and women would edge closer and closer and it wouldn't be long before you felt fingers moving through your hair. They only wanted to touch and feel a white person's long, straight hair. Wild? Indeed yes, but this is OUR continent: THIS IS AFRICA, remote, wild and still largely rural. There are multitudes upon multitudes in the valley of decision and how shall they hear without a preacher?

The heartbeat of God is for the nations of the world. Nobody can sit in the comfort and ease of his church and not be concerned with the lost and dying. If we carry the heartbeat of God, we must be burdened, concerned and troubled for those who have never heard, never seen the light. How long will the church continue to play games when the world is perishing? Do we really believe that the soul of one man is of inestimable worth? Do we really believe that each and every soul is as valuable to God as our own? Does the love and compassion of God so burn within us that, no matter the colour of a man's skin or the condition of his living, he is worthy to be saved and we are ready to do something about it? When God's heart burns into ours we can no longer be narrow-minded, short-sighted, jealous or fearful. An enlargement of soul takes place and we see through the eye of the Spirit the vast and desperate needs of perishing nations. Not only must it drive us to our knees but it must constrain us to do something about it.

Are we ready to be broken like bread to feed the hungry? Jesus ably demonstrated that the less bread He had the more He could feed. He's looking for individuals who will hear the cry of the nations of Africa. He does not need a vast multitude but of individual churches and persons who will be obedient. We are His hands, His mouth, His feet through which He reaches out to the great sea of peoples inviting them to "Come." Oh beloved, when the church has lost her holiness and righteousness, when she has lost the glory and her integrity she has lost her witnessing power.

It is high time for the churches of South Africa across the board to humble themselves before one another. It is incredible that the church recognises only two ordinances of the Lord Jesus when, in actual fact, there are three. We have all conveniently forgotten or brushed aside the ordinance of "foot-washing" and have relegated it to something "spiritual." But, indeed, Jesus humbled Himself and practically washed His disciples' feet with the command they were to wash one another's feet.

Oh that the world would see the humility and devotion of Christ Jesus lived out through His people. Black Christians cannot even get along with each other as much as white believers are suspicious and jealous of one another. However can we be reconciled inter-racially when we cannot work within our own groups? There is only one solution: PRAYER. It is prayer that oils the machinery and keeps the members flowing. Prayer breaks down the inner walls and exposes the facades setting men free from the prisons of their own making. Prayer brings churches back into communion with God and gives them the pulse-beat of His heart. Prayer cleanses, delivers and heals the joints of the body. Prayer puts back the fibre and fire. Prayer raises up the workers - Godly workers - for the fields which are white unto harvest. Prayer like nothing else, restores legitimacy to a lukewarm, careless people and revitalises a missionary vision.

The salvation of the South African church and nation is firstly REVIVAL and a natural expression of revival is missionary endeavour. May the rain of the Spirit begin to fall upon a nation that is filled with fear and has become hardened and callused by years of hurt, rejection and mistrust and replace it with compassion and love. The cry of the African nations is the Macedonian call to *"come and help."* The church in South Africa is filled with the Word but has no power. One of the tragedies of the South African church is that it has either locked itself into traditionalism or it has embraced the American "export." Much of what has been exported with American dollars is a corruption of the TRUTH. Self promotion and selfish ambition have pervaded the church. Visitors from America have brought their particular brands of doctrine and their "other gospels." Such teaching have found fertile ground in the affluent society of white South Africa which has become ensnared and luke warm.

Remember, it was the diamonds of Kimberly and the gold of the Rand that blinded the pioneering spirit of South Africa. Part of that pioneering spirit was the belief in a Divine mandate to preach the Word of God to the "heathen." Today multitudes of heathen still exist, but the pioneering spirit has been quenched by, *"The lust of the eyes, the lust of the flesh and the pride of life."* (1Jn 2:16). More than ever, it is time for the riches of South Africa to be used in fulfilling the high calling of God to take the Gospel to this vast Continent.

The years ahead are going to be a period of political jostling as new parties and a new government find their feet. May believers devote themselves to REVIVAL for the land and the greatest missionary endeavour South Africa has ever embarked upon. There is going to be raised up the offices of Apostle and Prophet as in the first century. It is time for Apostolic Government and authority to be established in the Church as there may be governmental disorder in the natural. *"The whole creation is groaning and travailing for the manifestation of the Sons of God."* (Rom 8:19). A son of God is one who is led totally by the Holy Spirit (Rom 8:4) and the "sons" are being kept from flowing in their full anointing by the current generation of spiritual leaders. Many well known leaders are failing to keep up-to-date with the moves of the Holy Spirit and they will pass on or be removed from office so that the flood of God's Apostolic power and authority may swamp the nations.

Beloved, don't quench the Spirit any longer. Be obedient to His stirrings which will prompt you into the service and high calling of the King. One of the things that God clearly told us when we started out in mission work twenty years ago was, "Use the little you have and as you are faithful, I will multiply it." At that time we were isolated Rhodesians whose passports were less acceptable then even South African's have been. Yet, despite every obstacle, the Lord began to take us to the nations because the nations were in our hearts.

One of the main keys to the survival of any church or fellowship is the depth or their missionary vision and Commitment. This is where the heart of God rests. His Spirit and blessings will be poured out on those who sacrifice for the cause of the lost. It is time to give ourselves, our money and our time for the nations of the world. South Africa has so much to offer: and God is not interested in "left-overs" or second best. The Lord takes pleasure in our giving when it hurts to give.

CHAPTER SIX

REVIVAL

People speak of a "sovereign" move of God, churches wait for it and communities long for it. There is no such thing as a sovereign move of God where His people are concerned. That's not to say that God is not sovereign and that He cannot move sovereignly should He so desire but He acts and reacts according to the heart cry of His people. Revival is a response to intercession: continual, persistent and persevering heart cries - wrenching cries - of God's people to *"Rend the heavens and come down."* (Is 64:1). By the very nature of desperation, hunger and accompanying agony, such wrestlings with God are not "funny ha ha" situations. True revival brings believers and non-believers alike into the presence of a Holy, awesome God who is still an all-consuming fire and in whose presence there must be a conviction of sin. He is the same God who came down upon Sinai's Mountain and shook it! He is the same God who caused Israel to tremble and who judged Korah and his princes in the Old Testament and Ananias and Sapphira in the New. Sadly modern teachings have demeaned God and brought Him to our level. He is not "Daddy," He is "Lord" and the very word "Lord" means omnipotent **DICTATOR**, the one who has power of life and death in His hands. Within the heart of fallen man is that persistent desire, planted by the enemy, that *"Ye shall be as gods knowing good and evil."* (Gen 3:5). That is precisely what the "Born Again Jesus" doctrine teaches in the end: that Jesus had to die spiritually and physically in hell and get born again. Thus, being the first fruits from the dead we then, like Him also get born again and are thus His equal. Such a belief which is actually the heart of one of the major movements today is nothing but a perpetration of what satan sold Eve in the garden. Jesus is not

"Buddy," He is LORD. He is only *friend* if I love Him and obey His commandments.

Knowledge puffeth up and the church has been guilty for the last two to three decades of an aggressive pursuance of knowledge. But, the Word declares, *"And I brethren, when I came to you, came not with the excellency of speech or of wisdom.... and my speech and my preaching was not with enticing* [seducing] *words of man's wisdom, but in the demonstration of the Spirit and of power...."* (1Cor2:1&4). We have substituted knowledge for power hence the glut on teaching. But, together with the plague of Judaism in the early church was the equal plague of "GNOSIS" or knowledge which Paul clearly declares as *another Gospel* which, *"Removes from the truth."*

Now while the church has aggressively pursued "knowledge" and has become an exclusive club, the lost are perishing. Revival is not some "Woo-wooooo" experience with God which is to give goose bumps - it does and I like the emotional experience - but a visitation of God to put His people back on track and substituting their agenda for His agenda. Like the Gospel, God's agenda for the individual is very clear and very, very simple: to love Him with my whole being. Out of such love will come a passion for the lost.

Many pastors would shout, "I'm in Revival! My church is having a revival." I say, "show me the fruit." The saddest thing today is that the church is so far removed from revival that very few people actually know what they are talking about. True Revivalists have a passion for God which transcends anything this world has to offer. "My car, my house, my retirement, my insurance benefit, my medical aid, my holiday," ad infinitum, pale into nothingness in the presence of a Holy God who demands to be worshipped. Look at what is bellowed from our pulpits: *WE* are going to take the land; *WE* are going to rise up.... *WE*.... *WE*.... *WE*.... *I*.... *I*.... *I*.... and *MY*.... *MY*.... *MY*.... Allow me to give a mini sermon. Most people avoid the book of Job - well, they avoid a lot of books in the Bible because they appear difficult to understand. But, like all things, we have to get the KEY. The key to Job is found in Chapter 29 and the problem is not the devil, it is Job himself and his pride. The Bible declares Job as a "righteous" man. Well, that's the average believer sitting in the average pew of the average church for whom everything is just fine. "I have my house, my car, my income, my family...." Compare yourself to Job 29 beloved. You see, despite the fact that people state that God wasn't responsible for all that happened to Job, *God gave* the devil license to do all that he did. There was the ultimatum - do as you will but spare his life. If you look at the judgement recommended to the Corinthian Church by Paul to, *"Deliver such a one to satan for the **destruction of the flesh,**"* (1Cor 5:5) it puts such a one in the same category as Job. Oh my, my it gets very interesting, doesn't it? Proverbs says, *"Pride goeth before destruction and a haughty spirit before a fall...."* (Prov 16:18). Oh but Job was *righteous*. Yes, as righteous as any believer today. He would have been a good, solid, Born-again denominationalist who paid his tithes and gave his offerings faithfully, attended church regularly and took his "perfect" family to lunch on Sunday at the Holiday Inn. He would drive his Mercedes or BMW and his wife would shop at Sandton or Eastgate and everything would be just fine and in Control. "I've made my little nest egg and I'm happy and content." Yes! But God is NOT!

    You see He called us to be radically in love with Him; so excited about Him that He is the all consuming passion of our lives so that our material things are mere incidentals. Blessings for which to be thankful but whether we have them or not will not make the slightest bit of difference to our relationship with God. Please don't get me wrong: there's nothing wrong with being rich, there's nothing wrong with having the good things and going to good places but if you lost it all, would your testimony be like that of Job's wife..... *"Curse God and Die."* (Job 2:9) or would there still flow from the inner recesses of your being that Zoe life which Jesus gave to the woman at the well? That's what joy is all about. It's not laughing or "funny ha, ha" but a deep seated relationship with Him which brings peace, such secure peace, the peace that passes all understanding so that we are unmoved by anyone and anything.   That is precisely why Paul declares that Righteousness + Peace = Joy. People are so set on struggling to be right; to overcome; to conquer habits, to be just so, that they miss the whole point. The whole point is Him! Him! Him! A thousand times it's Him! He is the RIGHTEOUSNESS: it's not a way or system or regulations or rules or set of achievements; He's a person - Jesus. He alone is our Righteousness, He is our peace and He becomes our Joy.

You shout, "Well that's me or my church." Yes, but is it the sum of the individuals and churches of South Africa? It is for this reason that there needs to be repentance. The only freedom and deliverance God can give is in repentance. At least righteous Job finally declares, *"I have heard of thee by the hearing of the ear; but now mine eye seeth thee. Wherefore I abhor **myself** and repent in dust and ashes."* (Job 42:5&6). That is precisely why REVIVAL is needed but true revival will not come until the CHURCH repents and begins to cry out for a visitation of God so that we might get back on track with Him. Actually, what is really required is an emotional experience with God. We have been brainwashed for years with the idea, "Don't walk by feelings, walk by faith." Sadly, this has brought our experience of God to the level of religious formulas. "Don't get too radical, too excited, too emotional." Friend, did you ever see anyone in love who was not emotional? God gave us our emotions and expects us to use them especially over Him. Of course I'm not talking about selfish, corrupted, carnal emotions of which we see so much and which terrifies people away from the real. Perhaps my favourite little song is :

> Lord I'm so in love with You
> Yes, I'm so in love with You
> Everything You are and everything You do
> Lord, I'm so in love with You.

Worship is relationship and there is almost a total absence of it in the church. We have substituted ACTIVITY for worship and embraced the ways of the world into the church.

Indeed revival is desperately needed but will never come because we "wish it or hope it in." It will come because a people will travail and weep until the attention of God is arrested and He gives that for which people are pleading. Is South Africa really pleading?

And what of the fruit of revival? Well, revival is a move and is very different from God giving a blessing; as different as a thunderstorm is from a shower of rain. I'm looking for the thunderstorms. Having once tasted REVIVAL nothing else will ever satisfy. It changes the heart, changes the life and changes our relationship with God forever. Above everything else Revival breeds within the ordinary believer a zeal, a fervour, a passion for the souls of lost men because it is the heart of God manifest to a lost and dying world. The very reason why the task of world evangelism is far lagging behind the population growth is because ordinary believers do not carry the burden of God. Evangelism has therefore been left to the specialist instead of being a natural expression of God's pulse-beat flowing through every vessel. The attitude, **"I'm saved. I'm fine"** does not express the nature of a loving, caring, compassionate God.

White South Africans of all denominations - and Pentecostals and Charismatics can be the worst - have sat in their ivory towers of "worship" with the money and resources to reach out and do something for those with less but have not deigned to stoop and soil their garments with such lowly aspirations. We forget that God Himself made Himself of no reputation and took upon Himself the form of a servant man; the lowliest bond-slave servant, that He might redeem man. Does anyone wonder why people are skeptical, have looked askance, felt rejected and become isolated and antagonistic? The apartheid that the church has practised and still practises is far more entrenched and disgusting than ever that practised by the State. It is all well and good to have discussions, pass resolutions and make moratoriums but unless we *DO* what Jesus said to do, all the good intentions are nothing but vain religion. There are monied ministries in South Africa that operate beyond the borders of the nation but do very little across the road, "in my own back yard" so to speak. I often wonder if such is not for publicity and effect and the budget.

I know of a very wealthy farmer in Zimbabwe. At a certain convention she was asked to be a "hand-maiden" to a certain faith preacher in the country. She was to book into the expensive Sheraton at her own expense and wait hand-and-foot on the whims of the preacher and his wife. The "silly" woman went "nuts" for weeks about the "honour" bestowed upon her. Sorry, but I think she was chosen because of her money and she pours oodles of money into the offering. But listen, I drive through her farm compound every time I visit my parents. The thatch on the roofs of her workers homes is worn, there's no electricity, no running water, no water-born sanitation. Get my point! Her religion is vain. Until she takes care of her own and shows the love of Jesus to those who earn her bread, butter and jam for her she's a hypocrite. The statement which I heard over and over from pastors in Mocambique during the worst years of Samora Machel's communism was, "Just because you've come we know that you care." I remember asking a pastor, "What can I bring you?" He replied,

"Nothing. We have been so long without things that we know how to live without them. But because you have come, we know that you love us. Just come again." That's enough to choke anybody to tears who has the heart of God.

Revival must cause one to look beyond oneself. Oh don't get me wrong. The coloured peoples of South Africa have been equally guilty. Until coloured peoples learn to give and suffer and sacrifice and shake off the intimidation and fear of the world and men they can never be the instruments God wants *them* to be. All too often coloured peoples put out the begging bowl. My good friend Nicholas Benghu once told me of an incident which happened to him as a young boy. He was in a trading store in his remote Zulu homeland. He said, "I asked my mother, 'Why mother do these shop owners call us Nikkers?'"

"Well," she replied, "it's like this. We black people hold out our hands like a bowl and say, 'Nika mina' and so they call us Nikkers."

So often in the mission work people come wanting me to build a church. Building is NOT really money, it's hard work. Sure I'll put on a roof and provide the cement but only after I see the bricks made and the sweat produced through hard work without which, nothing is achieved.

Revival must change all such entrenched habits and traditions by the introduction of the bigness of a BIG God. And above all, revival must give a compassion for the lost. There are only two things we are going to take out of this life with us: just how much we know Him and souls. I question any church which claims they are in revival and which does not have BOTH an aggressive local and trans-local missionary operation. Acts declares *"And ye shall be witnesses unto me **BOTH** in Jerusalem and in all Judea and in Samaria and unto the uttermost parts of the earth."* (Acts 1:8). The word "BOTH" means, "Together at the same time." How? By the fact that we are the glorious temple shining the living reality of an explosive Jesus who dwells within.

How far is South Africa from Revival? Sad to say, very far. Until every church of every denomination sets aside its agendas and programmes and normal services and begins to cry out to God - and I mean really cry and repent for coldness, lukewarmness, traditionalism and religion which has robbed God of the individual's true worship and prevented the Church from being the true light to the nation - there will never be change in the land. However can we expect the world to change if they do not see a change in us? However can South Africa fulfil her mandate unless she has the full backing of heaven to do so? Heaven will never back that which is shady, corrupt or wrong or is not the heartbeat of the author of all creation.

Revival must bring forth an army of men and women so filled with the power of the Holy Spirit that they will venture out into the worst, most hostile conditions to manifest the glory of God and plant His Kingdom in the nations.

CHAPTER SEVEN

IF MY PEOPLE

*A*LL South Africans of all colours are the victims of the society they have created. God's law is very clear: *"For whatsoever a man soweth that shall he also reap."* (Gal 6:7). Society looks upon sowing and reaping in material, tangible terms. But, there is reaping emotionally and mentally as well as physically.

Until the leadership of the ANC repent for the violence, intimidation and terrorism and apologise to South Africa, violence will continue in your land. I must say, at least white South Africa apologised for apartheid. If a "Truth Commission" is going to try a Magnus Malan it must also try a Winnie Mandela mainly for crimes against her own people. The Word of God is clear. *"They that take the sword shall perish with the sword."* (Matt 26:52).

I am convinced that it is for this reason that our African Continent is so ravaged by wars, coups and violence. There is a Biblical precedence in the Israelite bondage in Egypt. All too often Africa shouts about colonialism and the oppression under which they suffered. What rot. I have seen oppression, massacres and genocide in post-independent Africa which never existed under colonialism. Now, under apartheid, apart from out and out violence perpetrated mainly by black against black there was civil disobedience of every kind: strikes, non-payment of rents, power, water, school fees and so on. A whole generation of black South Africans have been *educated* into violence and civil disobedience. Suddenly that rebellious generation is told to stop and behave. Suddenly it is no more legitimate to shoot and necklace and burn and loot. Suddenly you are required to pay all your bills when you have lived off somebody else for the last decade.

Suddenly you cannot just do what you like, when you like and as you like.

Who really rules South Africa? The ANC have a majority in Parliament but sad to say it is a bunch of trade union cowboys and hooligans. Mr. Mandela, pay a visit to Mrs. Thatcher and learn how to smash the Trade Unions which now hold South Africa to ransom. You see, the Baby has become a monster - *"Spare the rod and spoil the child"* - which cannot now be controlled and which has purely selfish motives and ambitions and it is that which needs to be brought to order. It might well be a person's right to strike but it is not his right to intimidate others and nor is it his right to get paid for not working. God's Word is clear: *If any would not work, neither should he eat."* (2 Thess 3:10).

Now under the Egyptian bondage, Israel never resorted to violence - except Moses - nor civil disobedience. Nobody in Apartheid South Africa ever came anywhere near suffering the oppression and slavery of Israel in Egypt. But what did they do? *"The children of Israel **sighed** [not fought] by reason of the bondage, and they cried,* [no civil disobedience] *and their cry came up unto God by reason of their bondage. And God **heard** their groaning, and God remembered his covenant.... and God had respect unto them."* (Ex2:23&24)

Since the new Constitution, South Africa is a society that has gone crazy: crazy with sin. Proverbs expressly teaches, *"Righteousness exalteth a nation: but sin is a reproach to any people."* (Prov 14:34). The wave of sin held back for so long has come in and engulfed the entire nation: violence, pornography, corruption, immorality have suddenly become a way of life and an individual's right. I have lived and worked in many African countries with their various levels of bribery but never have had the experience I had recently at a South African border.

Without even asking me if I had anything to declare - I was exiting the country - the customs officer told me he wanted to search my vehicle. Fine. We went out and I opened the back and began to tell him what I had bought. I had nothing to hide. He showed no interest whatsoever. I was quite amazed. Looking at me he asked, "Don't you have a drink for me?" (He actually meant a soft drink).

"Sorry," I said, "I don't or I would gladly give you one."

"Well, what about money to buy one?" he asked. "You must have South African change? You won't need it over there."

I dug in my pockets and took out about eight Rand in coins and gave it to him. He walked away. A few days previously on entering at the same border post - it was a Saturday afternoon - the entire customs and immigration staff were drunk! Public servants, paid by public taxes were drunk on duty. "Oh, but it's their right under the new Constitution." Say anything and they'll strike citing harassment!

Now having said all so far, where am I going? Precisely to the fact that the whole South African situation is such a complexly interwoven web of sin that there is no point in blame-shifting, pointing fingers or accusing one another. It is time, and long overdue, that the whole nation repents for sin: whites against blacks, blacks against whites, coloured against Indian, blacks against Indians, whites against Indians, Indians against whites, and I have not finished the list! Do you get the point? It is so complex, that only God can unravel it. How is He going to do so? When the nation REPENTS.

Now the chances of a heathen State President calling the entire nation to a national day of REPENTANCE and PRAYER is a fat zero. Oh yes, I've heard all the way up in Central Africa that Mr. Mandela is supposed to be saved but I have never heard *him* confess that. My Bible says, *"Whosoever shall deny me before men, him will I also deny before My Father."* Saying the sinner's prayer alone does not save a man. A person really has to believe it and live it.

So then, what is the solution? The solution is no different than it has ever been. It is God's solution and God's solution is *HIS PEOPLE.*

If the Church points a finger and accuses and blame-shifts, however will the world know any different? The Church is God's barometer and standard. If that standard is corrupt, thereby what shall anything be measured? I'm not interested in men's opinions. I'm interested only in God's opinion and God's opinion is His Word which clearly states that there is, *"None righteous, no not one."* (Rom 3:10). Only Christ and His standard will ever work order and stability, harmony and blessing in any society. It is God's people who are called to manifest the glory and power of the Living Word as He is lived out through the believer's life.

*If **MY** PEOPLE which are called by My name, shall humble themselves and pray and seek My face, and turn from their wicked ways, then will I hear from heaven and will forgive their sin and will heal their land."* (2 Chron 7:14). I think everyone agrees that South Africa needs to be healed. If then, there is need for healing then there must be wickedness and sin. Where? Amongst "MY PEOPLE," says the Lord. You see, the Word is sure and we cannot negate it. We may not like what the Word has to say, we may squirm and duck and dive when the spotlight of the Word is upon us, but it is an absolute and will always speak the TRUTH.

The future of South Africa depends fairly and squarely upon God's people: of all denominations and organisations and colours. It is God's people who will ultimately be held accountable. People of God of South Africa, you have to get His vision in your heart; you have to have His mind in your soul instead of your own rebellious opinion. It is as simple as that.

Well, where does it all begin? It begins when I acknowledge as sin whatever I have done in the past or whatever opinion I have held which in any way contradicts the opinion of God. Believers need to stop holding on to and justifying their ideas and opinions and behaviour. If they do not line up with the Word of God, they are in sin. If they have no Biblical precedent they sin. If they deny a man's worth because of colour, race or culture they sin. If we do not love our brother we sin. If the compassion of Jesus does not flow through us but we say we are His, we are in sin. If we are afraid, jealous, angry or bitter we are in sin. If our eye is covetous because our brother has and we do not we are in sin. Isn't it amazing that Jesus said, "By this, shall all men know that you are my disciples....." Only one simple, unselfish act marks us out among men and manifests to the world what we really are: and it is LOVE. What a shortage of it there is in the Church. We are too involved with "our reputation and position" to love.

In Malawi there is a town called "Nsanje" which means jealousy. Oh my, did I ever see people being jealous of one another and some of the worst culprits were those who named the name of Jesus. That's sin. If I have a business and practise corrupt methods, backhanders, pay-offs, bribes, it's sin. If I hate my brother because he's a Xhosa and I'm a Zulu it's sin.

It is time to stop excusing and making excuses for the national sins that plague South Africa. The immorality, lust and violence are only indicative of a far greater cancer that has eaten away inside and caused that muscle atrification of the marathon runner which zaps his strength and prevents him from running the race. "Bafana Bafana" and the national rugby team are not going to unite the nation. Monday morning realism is not wiped away because of a euphoric Saturday afternoon of emotionalism.

Jesus would ask, "Have you done what I told you to do?" And, until that happens men's religion is vain. I will tell you what I want to see and it is in line with His Word. I want to see Archbishop Tutu take an towel and basin of water and literally wash the feet of the Moderator of the Dutch Reformed Church. Are you above Jesus that you should not do such a thing? Why in that order you might ask? Because the Bishop has been so vociferous and critical of the white knights, spewing forth vitriolic rhetoric over the years which is totally unbecoming both his office and the name of the Lord Jesus Christ. I want to see some of the big name white preachers put a basin and towel in their fancy cars and drive across town to the high density suburbs and wash the feet of some black pastor who struggles to make ends meet, battles to keep his church together against incredible odds and prays and fasts for heaven to be shaken and revival to come. I do not want that same pastor to go with a paternalistic attitude of bestowal but in the humility of Jesus with Christ's love burning in his heart and see and realise that some COLLEAGUES, fellow-labourers in the vineyard, really do have it tough.

I remember as a very young minister barely in my twenties, I was assigned a church with a notoriously bad reputation. I heard later that the joke in the denomination was that, "If any pastor could survive......... then he would make it." Well, I had to work and pastor but I was so in love with Jesus that nothing mattered. Each month I gave 90% of my salary to the Church to get her out of debt and keep her operating. Nobody asked me to, nobody knew I did and at the time, nobody would have cared. But there was a need and as a single, young teacher living in a hostel with everything provided, God's need was greater than my want and I was pleased - no - honoured to be used. Furthermore, it was the harsh war years in Rhodesia. My allocation of fuel under rationing was six units (a unit was five litres) per month. We had a prayer meeting at least three times a week at 5.00 a.m. I would rise at 4.00, run all the way to the church (about five miles away) pray for an hour and run back to the hostel in time for school at 7.30 a.m.

There was only one thing that I wanted. I wanted my brother, my colleague, my fellow-labourer with his big and successful church to walk up to me at the ministerial conventions and ask, "How are you doing? How is the work going?" He never did. He was always too full of his church, his travels and what God was doing and saying in and through his life. I wasn't even asking him to come down to my neck of the woods.

Then suddenly one day the denominational "hero" arrived. I was overwhelmed, honoured, humbled. I had never been good enough for him but here he was in person: travelled the 250 kilometres to come especially to see me. I wanted to take the man of God to lunch, buy him a gift, show my appreciation for his love, his care, his concern and his Christ-like nature. But, I had no money: it was all in the church. To give the man his due, he did ask how the church was doing but he had not come for that. He was campaigning for a higher role on the executive committee and needed my vote! That's the ONLY reason he had come. He never got it!! I did not allow that to shatter or disillusion me but I certainly marked it.

When I became the leader of a work I made sure that I always had time for the "Little Man:" to eat a meal with him, drop a note of encouragement, visit his family, drop some money in an envelope, attend his child's wedding, preach in his little mud church.

I travelled to South Africa recently to see a big name preacher. No, I wasn't there to ask for money. One preacher said, "I suppose you've come for money, all you missionaries are the same!" It is about time the church HIGHLY honoured missionaries instead of relegating them to the gutter.

"Well," the big name said, "I don't have time to see him."

"But he's come all the way from Central Africa - Rwanda in fact."

"Too bad, I'm too busy." That same man would be too busy to see Jesus if He'd walked into the suite of offices too. If Pastor Big Name was too busy to see me then he'd most certainly be too busy to drive across town to see Pastor Nobody in some run down church. Jesus says, *"Have you done what I told you to do?"*

I grumbled one time when one of my pastors awoke me at 1.00 a.m. I get a lot of that kind of stuff. A woman in the local high density area was in child-birth and haemorrhaging. Would I take her to the hospital?

"Why me?" I questioned the pastor. "Why do they always come to me?"

"Because nobody else will help them," he replied.

That's why the "nobody" pastor in Mocambique said, "We know that you love us because you came."

I'm not a hero; just in love with Jesus and seeking to do His will.

There has got to be a humbling, a crying out to God, a seeking of His face. When Israel did so in Egypt God not only heard, but He respected it. If God's people will :
1. Humble themselves.
2. Pray! Pray!! Pray!!!
3. SEEK His face, His opinion, His desire.
4. Turn from selfishness and greed.

Then, God will hear from heaven and forgive and HEAL the land.

Church, you cannot expect the world to do it. They know no differently. It begins with us and the longer we take the harder it will be and the more entrenched sin will become. The future of South Africa is in the hands of the Church. If she does nothing it is a shame, a mockery, a blight on the name of Jesus. I know some are walking with Christ and in the way He told us to. God bless you as you honour Him and show His love in real practical terms to a dying world. But it is going to take the majority; the whole army of God to rise up and be what God has called us to be, to effect change.

Come on Dutch Reformed Church: your forefathers built a nation from their ox-wagons whether anyone likes it or not. Now it's time to build the Kingdom of God throughout Africa and you can do it.

CHAPTER EIGHT

EXPORTED RELIGION

I am very intolerant of Third World religious leaders who claim that Jesus is a western God and that to embrace Him means to adopt western culture. Not at all. But, what people must realise is that the West has had the Gospel for centuries and so the culture of the West *should*, in fact, be the culture of Christianity. As a missionary to the Third World, it is neither my mandate nor my calling to change anyone's culture. I preach "Christ and Him crucified" and allow the convicting power of the Holy Spirit to change people's culture. Of course, much of the Third World culture *has* to be changed because by its very nature it has been established around the occult.

Now then, one of the biggest problems - and it is far bigger than anyone has imagined or understood - which faces Africa and particularly South Africa, is the American Gospel Enterprise. I will speak the truth but from the outset I want you to know that I love preaching in America, I have many dear friends there and I openly share my views with them. The Gospel in America has to be marketed like all other goods and services. People in America for the most part are no longer moved only with a passion for souls and compassion for the lost. Giving in many places, is on the basis that I will get something in return. It is for this reason that the "Prosperity Gospel" has been successful in America. There is both a blatant and subtle underlying motive, "What's in it for me?" Sad to say, the inestimable worth of a man's soul is not sufficient. People want tangible, material returns.

I have been told many times in America, "But you have a unique ministry. If you'll only just do it the right way (they mean the American way) you'll become famous; we can really market you."

One dear pastor friend who is very successful told me, "Oh get real. This is the 20th Century. Market yourself."

Another big evangelist told me, "Quit wasting your time trying to move Americans with a compassion for Rwanda. Sell it to them. Offer them something and they'll go for it."

It is precisely for this reason that many Christian television projects offer, "My latest book free for your gift of $10, $20, $50." Or, "For those of you who would like to, you may join our Gold Club Membership. We are offering you....." "get this it's unbeatable, it's incredible, it's a once-in-a-lifetime offer....." "If you get this gold plaque with our emblem on it which you can proudly display.... and yes, you cannot believe it - it's not all, there's a free weekend package for you and your wife at our all exclusive Golden Sands Hotel: that's a completely free weekend all for your donation of $1,000. Come on folks, that's unbeatable value. There's the 'phones now: look, people are calling in from all across the country. Don't miss this unique chance. Limited space available so make your call now. There is only limited Gold Card membership so call right away and make that commitment to this incredible ministry vision to open this park and save the great Indian tiger in the name of Jesus. What a testimony it will be....!" And, the lost are going to a Christless Eternity while people play religious power games.

I have been told many times, "You preach too tough! Tone it down; give the people a placebo and they'll love you and really give to your ministry." So it has become an issue of marketing technique and we send our young to colleges and universities to study business so that they can market the Gospel, the result being that we "BUSINESS" the Holy Spirit clear out of His Word. We belong to too many *clubs* and not a Kingdom; a *corporation* and not The Body, and *organisation* and not the living organism of pulsating life. The big time preacher is a CEO who must be in competition with the rival corporation down the street: and, it's all a question of money. I heard recently in Johannesburg that the pastors of two large churches will not even speak to each other and have a tacit agreement not to have the same guest speaker. If that's true, it's shame on the church. One of them - I don't care which - needs to take a bowl of water and wash the other's feet and say, "Brother, I'm wrong, please forgive me"

This is all Gospel Enterprise in operation: kill or be killed. If that's what it has become it is no better than the big business corporations of the world. The real root of the great P.T.L. scandal in America in the late '80's was nothing less than P.T.L. having cornered the greater portion of the "market" in the Corporate Christian business world. The dog fight was on! The other Christian Media Moguls could never let such a thing happen so it was a case of "kill" Jim Bakker and the P.T.L. Corporation. The sordid, sad, sequel is public knowledge.

The church in South Africa is running the same dangerous tightrope. Being an affluent society, South Africa has naturally attracted the American Gospel Enterprise. But, with the exportation of American dollars has been the exportation of a religious system which is an Ishmael and not an Isaac, a bastard and not a true son. "Wow," you say, "true," I say. Pick up any South African Christian Magazine and what do you see advertised: tapes from America, books from America, music from America and messages and speakers from America. Now don't get me wrong. I am not saying that there aren't good preachers and teachers and books, tapes and music in America. Many I come across are excellent BUT, there are African preachers of all races who have really paid a price and preach and teach equally as well but they're nobodies because they're not in the corporation. What I'm saying through all this is that South Africa is becoming swallowed up by America and is no more uniquely African. Her eyes gravitate to America and not Africa. It is easier and more lucrative to be in the Corporation, say the right thing, play the religious game and get marketed. Now of course, the preaching of the Gospel takes money and people have to have money but we are supposed to get wealth for one purpose: to propagate the Gospel. I find more and more that the Church ministers to the Church displaying that "Club mentality," without reaching the lost.

A very big international preaching friend of mine told me, "The only place in Africa that I can afford to go is South Africa because that is where the money is."

See friends, African preachers are uniquely anointed probably because they've been through the fire; they've known how to pray and fast and they have really taken hold of God who in turn has taken hold of them. Sometimes or should I say oft-times, we African preachers have no finesse or methodology. So, somebody sees the potential and markets us. Before long we have sold ourselves to the Corporation. There has been a continental spiritual drain from Africa and yet, there is still a whole continent hungry and waiting to be developed spiritually. The call of South Africa is to *this* continent and not America. South Africa has the resources, the capabilities and the spiritual power to reach Africa but she has become enamoured with America. African preachers are really "making it" in America but sadly, few send those resources back to Africa to really reach this continent. The potential for ministry in Africa is enormous but believe me there is very little money north of the Limpopo. One has to be a tent-maker as well. Plenty of money is available in tent-making in Africa but it needs men to tap into those resources for the Kingdom of God and not their own selfish ambition.

With American dollars there's often strings attached because it's business: "Preach my way, believe what I believe; teach my teachings and I will support you." If not directly said, it is tacitly implied and you will know pretty soon if you're not performing up to requirement or expectation. The problem is that we are African with African culture - much of which needs changing, yes - and must establish our own models for the African context.

What really upsets me is that wherever I am going in the African countries these days, I find South African businessmen: from Dar-es-Salaam to Kinshasa to Quelimane to Addis-Ababa and Kampala. In cities and in remote areas South African businessmen have moved their operations with a swiftness that is amazing. But where are the Christians? Where are the missionaries? Where are the people of God? You mean to say Assemblies of God, Full Gospel, AFM, Baptist, IFCC, Dutch Reformed that you cannot send forth from your organisations bands of fully equipped and supported missionaries? Is it that we just don't care or don't know how to go about it or is it because the South African Church is too wrapped up in what happens in the U.S.A., the media image, the Corporate Church?

I was recently in Pretoria discussing filming with a church media boffin. The gentleman was pointedly asked, "What is your organisation doing in the mission fields?" His answer blew me away but it is the acceptable cliché today. "Oh," said he, "we don't believe in sending out teams of missionaries. They don't work. They eat a lot of money and there is no fruit from the investment. Consequently we have decided to invest all our missionary budget in building a television station....in Lusaka."

Excuse me, but let's test that against God's Word and not my opinion or anyone else's opinion. No matter how good mass media may be - and there are many advantages - God ordained that the Gospel be preached through vibrant, living Epistles. Men cannot read a radio or a television but the greatest missionary of the Church Age, Paul the Apostle, declares, *"You are our epistle written in our hearts, known and read of all men: forasmuch as YE are manifestly declared to be the epistle of Christ ministered by us, written not with ink but with the Spirit of the Living God not in tables of stone, but in fleshly tables of the heart."* (2 Cor 3:2&3).

Jesus Himself said "Go *ye*....." but our modern age has found it sufficient to substitute the "ye" with a radio, television, film or video.

They are good aids but it must always be remembered that they are nothing more than aids. Why has the church substituted them? Simply because it is convenient. It requires less effort and input to show a Jesus movie than preach a powerful Gospel message. The problem with media ministry is that souls become a mere number or statistic instead of being a living organ which is to be shaped into the image of Christ. That can never be done by radio or television but only by vessels who really know Him and are like Him. It is for this reason that some of the greatest evangelists of our generation are beginning to question their results and go so far as to suggest failure in their ministries over significant decades.

When a church or mission organisation suggests that sending forth a missionary family or group has been a waste of finances and time it is really declaring that the vessels are ill-equipped and that *they* have failed. The methodology has been formulated by the Holy Spirit and I do not care if it is the 23rd Century, His methodology cannot and will not ever fail. His methodology is clearly manifest in the Acts of the Holy Spirit operating through vessels which were dead, dead, DEAD to self and dynamically ALIVE to Jesus. Sadly today, we send out highly educated, *soul* equipped men and women who do not KNOW the Holy Spirit, His ways or His power. How many missionaries have ever done a 40 days or 21 days, 10 days or even 3 days water fast. How do we ever think we can march into some of the strongholds of satan and be effective if we do not know how to fast and pray? I do not care how long a person spent in college, how much faith he has been taught, how much prosperity he knows or any other of the new-fangled "gospels" have been bombarded into his life; if He does not radically love Jesus and show it and demonstrate the power of the LIVING PERSON of the Holy Spirit, he is, indeed, wasting his time and the organisation's money. Our two year Bible School Programmes at our local churches often taught by lecturers who themselves are not equipped, give a lot of theory and very little practical experience of the Living Dynamic of Jesus

I have ministered in Tanzania and seen missionary after missionary collapse at the hands of the Masai. The Masai are purported to have descended from the Romans which explains their shields, spears and the typically Roman red and purple capes. The Emperor Nero sent a Roman expedition across the Sahara. It never returned but reports came back that a remnant of the expedition reached East Africa where the men intermarried with the local tribeswomen and a new regal breed of people was established. The Masai are very aggressive and warlike. They are a blood-drinking people and will often drink fresh blood directly from the veins of their living cattle. With such and other heathen practises which directly violate God's Word, this huge tribe stretching from Southern Kenya to Southern Tanzania are bound by very strong forces of darkness. The typical tactic of the Masai with missionaries is to have them compromise their faith. They will often agree to let missionaries into the tribe "if you only...." The compromise extends from initiation rites, to drinking blood mixed with milk to intermarrying. The endless list does nothing but rob the missionary of any power thereby rendering such totally ineffective before the heathen. Natives are not interested in hearing theoretic messages on faith and prosperity learned at some Church Bible School. They want to see that the God we serve is stronger than all the gods they serve. They need to see the powers that enslave: fear, sickness, witchcraft, broken and replaced with love, Divine health and peace.

Sending out teams of young inexperienced "whipper-snappers" is a mockery. I see from years in the field that most people today want an adventure. But, Paul declares to the Thessalonians,

"So being affectionately desirous of you, we were willing to have imparted unto you, not the Gospel of God only, but also our own souls, because ye were dear unto us." (1 Thess2:8).

What is needed is for men and women filled with the living dynamic of Jesus Christ and the Holy Spirit to be willing to go into the inner cities; into the remote tribal areas, into the most hostile of places and be ready both to live and if necessary, die radiating Jesus before the people. The Church is losing the battle in world evangelism - despite all our modern methods and equipment - because we have chosen our way above God's way. What is God's way? The way of the Cross, the way of death. It is for this reason that Islam is on the march. Let me blast a real dampener on the euphoric unity spirit which has exploded on South Africa. Allah is NOT Jehovah but a demon prince and the reason why Moslems world-wide are making such inroads is because they are ready to die for what they believe. Sadly, unlike our first century namesakes, we Christians are far from ready to die for Jesus let alone live for Him. It is for this reason and this reason alone that the Gospel is lagging far behind percentage wise not only world population increase but also cultic increases.

Only when the Church returns to its roots and the methodology of the Book of Acts and obedience to our Captain's command, *"Go YE, YE, YE"* will the Church be triumphant as she is supposed to be. God chose you as a vessel to take His Life, encased in a frail human frame, to Jerusalem, Judea, Samaria and the uttermost parts. There is no such thing as short term missions. Missions is a life-time investment to those who have never experienced Jesus. Few, very few, today are prepared to invest that life-time where there may be little to no tangible rewards.

CHAPTER NINE

THE SOCIAL GOSPEL

Let's get it straight no matter how unpalatable it might be. Jesus said, *"Go ye..... and preach **THE** Gospel."* Most Christians do not even know what **THE GOSPEL** is. I have never asked that question without the answer, "Good News," being returned. Yes, that's the meaning of the word but that's not the Gospel. Paul emphatically declares, *"I marvel that ye are so soon removed....unto another gospel....but there be some that would pervert the Gospel of Christ."* The word "pervert" means to modify or water down by adding something thereto. Paul continues, *"But though we, or an angel from heaven, preach **and other gospel** unto you than that which we have preached unto you, let him be accursed,"* or cut off and destroyed. (Gal 1:1-8). That is strong wording. In 2 Cor 11:4, Paul warns against those who preach *"another Jesus," "another spirit,"* and *"another gospel."*

Be warned friend: if any type of Christianity you are experiencing has become complex, complicated, debatable or difficult to understand, it is not of God. The Bible speaks of the simplicity of Christ, the simplicity of the Gospel and the simplicity of the Word. So then, what is THE GOSPEL which is a TRUST unto us? In a nutshell Paul declares in 1Cor 15:1-4 the Gospel and the only Gospel which saves men. There is no other Gospel.

"But," you say, "Why have you headed this chapter 'The Social Gospel?' Surely you are splitting hairs over terminology?" Indeed NO, when you consider the word, "PERVERTED" means to water down or become luke warm. I believe that the Laodician Church has become "luke warm" for the very reason that they, like so many today, had increased with wealth and knowledge and thereby perverted *the Gospel* with men's innovations.

Today the Church has been deceived, seduced and perverted into another gospel, the so-called "Social Gospel." Nowhere, absolutely nowhere in the Word are we commanded to embark on a social gospel. A social gospel cannot save a man: never has and never will. No indeed, the church has again followed the way of the world and become another "social welfare agency." Why? To go with the flow, to stem off criticism, to be acceptable and to raise money. To merely preach THE GOSPEL is no longer socially acceptable and deemed of no value. It is the responsibility of the local church to take care of the widows and orphans not for the church to embark on a social gospel.

Now listen. I have been preaching THE GOSPEL for twenty-five years in the Third World. I have seen the U.N. and every kind of World Agency pour vast billions into one refugee camp after another and I have seen one Church or religious organisation after another follow suit in a copy-cat way. Why? Because for the most part, it is where the money is. But, in twenty-five years of ministry I can honestly say I have never seen humanitarian aid, refugee programmes or anything to do with the social gospel save a man spiritually. I have even worked with powerful evangelistic organisations that have pumped millions into social gospel programmes until my heart has broken with the waste and abuse of finances but never seen a soul won for Jesus. I have seen Christian orphanages from Mocambique to Zimbabwe to Tanzania and Rwanda and India that operate under a name and veneer of Christianity but are really no different to worldly orphanages and which do not seek to save the soul but only the life. I have watched horrified, as Christian Aid Organisations have given out food and clothing but never preached the Gospel along with it. I have been in the camps across Africa where the only thing I saw was containers sent by well-meaning Christians cause hatred, confusion, division and jealousy amongst the very believers intended to be helped.

I have heard the pleas of Christian leaders in refugee camps not to send material assistance; YES, *not* to send material assistance because of the trouble it creates.

So then, why is the Church so eager to embark on a social gospel? Why are believers so willing to plough in food, clothes, buildings and all kinds of often, obsolete material provisions? The real reason is because we are not willing to give OURSELVES.

Christians today are more than eager to give things and not themselves, to give of a little time and not their lives, to give money and not to go. Then of course there is the ulterior motive. It is easy to play on the soul emotion of people's conscience strings and have them give to XYZ orphanage project. I pick on orphanages because they are the biggest money spinners today. Because people no longer freely give to THE GOSPEL, moneys have to be raised "deceitfully." People will gladly give to the building of an orphanage especially when they see photographs of little babies crying or injured. I watched, horrified, as a TV evangelist appealed for finances for an orphanage in Rwanda. He challenged 1,500 people to give $1,000 each and had the money within days. Anyone who knows Africa and particularly Rwanda at this time knows it does not take even a 1/4 of that to build an effective orphanage. The rest??????????? Yet at the same time another organisation sent out over two thousand video tapes showing footage of the Rwandan refugee camps and stating any finances raised would not be used for food, clothing or medical supplies but to preach the Gospel. They received only two replies and $1,180. That is frightening. I personally know someone who was the associate director of a large evangelistic ministry involved in the social gospel programme in a certain African nation and it was a major battle for that person to get even the smallest percentage of the vast budget released for the purchase of Bibles and literature to hand out with the food most of which was just dumped in warehouses in the various refugee camps. We have seen thousands of bags of wheat and maize in those warehouses infested with weevils. The Gospel was never preached with the donation of food, clothing, or whatever. Why am I saying all this now? Because the white South African Church with all its wealth is in danger of being side-tracked especially in their endeavours to "apologise" for apartheid and make amends. Freedom comes only through REPENTANCE and once there has been true repentance, their is no more guilt.

Christian you are called to PREACH the saving power of a resurrected Jesus who is the only name under heaven to bring salvation. Any social programme must be a minute aid to the main focus of preaching THE GOSPEL. To this end we live and to this end we should be ready to die: that men might hear the good news that only Jesus saves and that Jesus is God in the flesh and lives forever.

The governments of the world cannot even begin to take care of the vast needs which are mostly created by the sinfulness of fallen man. The Church must get back on track and into focus. South Africa, you were made rich and powerful to preach the Gospel to this vast continent. Unbelievable doors are now open to South Africans to take their knowledge and expertise throughout the African Continent and with that must go the Gospel. African nations are waiting and ready to receive THE TRUTH. Anything short of this is a travesty.

Do I believe in a school, a clinic, an orphanage. Only in so far as they are going to be the most dynamic testimonies and living expressions of the power of THE GOSPEL. But, if it is because it is the socially acceptable thing to do, forget it. I have seen denominational hospitals, schools, clinics and orphanages across Africa which have never changed the lost heart of anyone. I have seen born again, spirit filled doctors, nurses, teachers and a whole gamut of professionals so caught up in their professions that they simply have no time or are too exhausted by the social needs of the multitudes to minister the dynamic life of Jesus to them.

Jesus Himself must be our yardstick. It is He and He alone we must emulate. He told us to, *"Go..... PREACH to every creature."* He said, *"But ye shall receive power......"* that power not just to preach but to LIVE CHRIST. So few believers today actually LIVE CHRIST hence the fact that we have such poor testimonies. Jesus said, *"...And ye shall be witnesses unto Me **BOTH** in Jerusalem, and in all Judea and in Samaria, and unto the uttermost part of the earth."* As I said before, "BOTH" means "together at the same time." How is this to be achieved? The Church has largely become stilted and devoid of life because we quench the enthusiasm of men and women who are truly called. Because the ulterior motive is to keep the rich, talented or gifted believer in the Church and not send them forth, we prevent others from rising up to operate in their gifts and talents. A "bottle neck" effect is created and one of the outlets is the social gospel: donate a few hours of service; build a school, fill a container of clothes; keep the aspirant out of mischief and certainly out of the pulpit. Yet, the early church gave her very best sons and daughters to the mission fields of the world. Paul was "sent" which is what missionary work is all about.

Success today is measured in terms of buildings, numbers, budgets. Now all that can measure success but the absence of it does not necessarily mean lack of success. Upon whose standard are we measuring? Paul emphasises that, *"I have planted, Apollos watered; but God gave the increase. So then neither is he that planteth any thing, neither he that watereth; but God that giveth the increase..... for we are labourers together with God...."*

The young man in Pretoria missed the whole point of mission work. Paul was up to three years in some places. Sometimes results are very slow and it is literally a question of, *"He that goeth forth and weepeth, bearing precious seed, shall doubtless come again with rejoicing, bringing his sheaves with him."* (Ps 126:6). God is not in a hurry and sometimes it takes much time, effort and finances to establish the Kingdom and see change. In a small museum in northern Malawi at Livingstonia there is a record of the work of some of the early missionaries. One such record has been drawn up in the form of a profit and loss account. It reads something like this:

1. 6 missionaries sent   5 Dead
2. 3 years work   2 Converts
3. 2,000 pounds spent   Mission closed

But today, there exists a powerful work which has changed the whole of northern Malawi. Indeed, the Blood of the Martyrs *is* the seed of the Church.

In whatever way a person is won, that is usually how he is kept. It is for this reason that rap, rock and metal music have become so popular in the church: to attract and keep the young people. But, there is no substitute for the pure Word and honest hard preaching, teaching and praying.

Only Jesus can save a man for eternity. We may feed and clothe men, educate them and do a whole lot of other things but still send them to a Christless eternity. Men may win human accolades for their humanitarian service but not a word from God. Church, it is time to return to your roots: it is time to so burn with a love for Jesus, be so fired with His vision and so fearful of disobeying His commands that nothing, absolutely nothing, will stop us from going forth with His Word under the power of His anointing to change Africa by His Word.

CHAPTER TEN

CRY FOR HELP

The Macedonian cry, *"Come over into Macedonia and help us,"* is a cry that has gone up from Africa. It is not so much that Africans want money, they want people. But, they must be the right calibre and quality people. Many times my African pastors have said, "Pastor don't bring........ here again. He does not love us. All he wants are our pictures so that he can make money out of us...."

It was shortly after the Rwandan genocide that the Lord clearly directed me to go up to that crisis area to spy out the land in prelude for something bigger. It was very inconvenient at the time and so I began to make a few paltry excuses like, "Lord I don't have the finances!" No sooner had I said such than somebody sent $1,000 specifically for me to go to Rwanda. Having settled that the tyres on my vehicle were so bald, the canvas was showing. The Lord challenged me by asking, "How long were the children of Israel in the wilderness?"

"Forty years, Lord," I replied.
"Did their shoes ever wear out?"
"No Lord."
"Then," he replied, "If I could keep the children of Israel for forty years, I can keep your tyres from wearing out on a journey to Rwanda and back."

He did! We travelled about 10,000 kilometres and those tyres never wore and further. We experienced only two punctures which is miraculous considering some of the most hostile terrain through which we had to travel often without any kind of road at all.

I've been in war, I have experienced prison and refugees up and down Africa but there was something terrible and extra tragic about the

Rwandan refugees and their vast sprawling camps housing millions of destitute.

After the initial investigations we moved up to the camps some months later for a spiritual onslaught. Our friends told us we would be killed, other missionaries called us crazy, the Government of Tanzania warned us to have armed guards and the United Nations declared us *persona non grata* from the outset. The Jezebel U.N. director was nothing less than God hating and instructed all aid organisations to, "have nothing to do with them and give no assistance to them whatsoever." How different it would have been if we had toted along containers of food, medicines and clothing. But we were there to preach THE GOSPEL and told in no uncertain terms that, "We don't want you types here." That was the initial introduction and welcome which spelled that things could only get worse; and they did!

How my heart broke for the people: sheep without a shepherd. The few believers whom we met were widely scattered and told us that we were the first and only missionaries who had taken up residence. Others indeed had come "to get pictures," they said. Most of the missionaries preached a few quick messages mainly along the theme, "REPENT you murderers, thieves and liars," before fleeing off to Nairobi or Dar-es-Salaam. Many refugees poured out their hearts about the genocide, the hatred, the conditions and the fact that being mainly Hutu they were all labelled murderers. Yet, we watched in horror as the same barbarity was executed upon the Hutu by the Tutsi and the U.N. and the world said nothing.

Even "Time" Magazine declared that if the world continued to stand idly by and do nothing, God was going to judge us. Time and again we were told by Christian leaders in the camps not to bring food and clothing. "Well," I asked, "If there is one thing, just one thing, which you people would have me bring, what would it be?" Without hesitation, the reply returned unanimously was, "A Bible School." The believers wanted to be taught such subjects as reconciliation, how to intercede, spiritual warfare. I taught on knowing the enemy. Oh what enlightenment and hope began to burst upon those leaders as they realised the nature and purposes of satan and just how he had used the differences between the Hutu and Tutsi to utterly destroy one another.

We spent months in the camps pouring out our lives in love, giving some hope to the hopeless and experiencing the full force of satan's anger unleashed upon us by the U.N. which was a willing pawn in the enemy's hands.

But, it was through the U.N. that I also saw what could be achieved when people work together. Of course, they worked with an almost limitless budget but money does not always achieve everything. I marvelled at how they moved in with bulldozers and set up whole supply depots using enormous tents.

It was there that God spoke of the need for an international task force of Christians just for such crises which He declared would become more numerous in the future. The Kingdom of God has the material, has the resources and has the manpower to do something about it. I experienced a whole gamut of emotions from horror to nausea to frustration to anger as I gazed upon the enormous needs and considered the Church playing religious games while the world is dying. Never in the history of Central Africa was there such an opportunity to reach so many in such a short space with really such a little expenditure. The problem is friends, we are all glory seeking instead of Christ seeking. Here was a prime case for the South African Church: Blacks, whites, coloureds, Indians, Afrikaans, English of all denominations saying we will lay aside our differences which have sadly become DIVISIONS to address a need which is vastly beyond the capability of any one group to address.

The South African Church has the resources to change Rwanda. If the whole Church would rise up and literally bombard the Tutsi in Rwanda with the love of Jesus and bombard the Hutu in the camps in the same fashion, the Church, yes the Church, could lead the Hutu home and establish a nation of peace and love. The effort is massive but not beyond the capabilities and resources of the South African

Church. It would be nothing to set up tent villages to include full Bible Schools with teams moving in and out on a regular basis. A three month stint in the camps would change most people's lives forever. What are all those Christians doing who boast high level contacts with Government? They could easily have mobilised transport planes, army equipment and a whole mobile force of Christians who would literally overwhelm the camps with love, literature and teaching.

I went to Kabwe, Zambia and agonised as I saw part of Pastor Bonnke's huge tent being used once-a-week as a struggling church. I realised that some enterprising Zambian had sweet-talked somebody into getting such a facility and then had not the resources to utilise it properly. We had wept for just such a facility for the camps in Rwanda. Our pleas fell on deaf ears. Everybody was too busy with his own programme. Well, I had been busy with mine too, but here was an international crisis - here IS an international crisis for it has not been solved and will not go away - of major proportions which needs the attention of the whole Church of South Africa. Look beyond yourself South Africa. Mobilise a Christian army. Do something that can be written in the annals of Eternity. At least send in a task force to see what can be done, what must be done. It's time to sow where there might be no reaping and to give where there might be no material return.

Nero played fiddle while Rome burned and the Church is playing religion, politics and power games while the Continent implodes. Where is the Church of Andrew Murry? Where is the Church of Nicholas Benghu? Where is the Church of John G. Lake? Where is the Church of the Mullans brothers? It is time for every leader to get enflamed with the vision of the Holy Spirit again, have the courage to break forth from the mould that encapsulates and to have the strength to mount a Holy Ghost offensive against the onslaught of hell.

The Church in South Africa *is* a sleeping giant which needs to stir and rise up conquering and victorious instead of being tied like a

Gullivar by the myriads of little cords of an army of dwarves. Social programmes and niceties, religious bondage, doctrinal arguments, selfish ambition and material gain - to name but a few factors - have robbed the Church of power and stilted her growth.

It is suddenly fashionable to minister in Zambia because of a Christian President. But, where was the Church during the darkest days of Kaunda? It suddenly became the vogue to visit Robben Island during the last couple of years before the great changes, but what about all those proceeding years? What I am saying is that now is the time to emerge from our comfort zones and do something that will impact not only South Africa, but the whole of this very needy continent. Where was the Church when there was wholesale persecution and slaughter in Mocambique? Where was the Church when communism had overrun Ethiopia? Where is the Church in the southern Sudan crisis? Where is the Church in Rwanda and Burundi? We can no longer stand idly by and do nothing. South Africa has been liberated and now the Church in South Africa must stop looking overseas to America, to Europe, to Australia and start to look to the vast needs of her own Continent.

There is a very powerful Biblical Principle in the fact that though personal needs may be great, in addressing the vast needs of others outside the personal realm God will automatically take care of personal needs. That is what it is all about: when we are commanded **BOTH** to Jerusalem, Judea, Samaria and the uttermost parts all at the same time we are looking beyond the often enormous needs of the home front to sacrifice on behalf of others. Where true sacrifice exists, God finds it very pleasing and a miracle is done. The national needs of South Africa are enormous and have not even begun to be met. However, if the Church would address the cry of the Continent to, "Come over and help us," God will hear the cry of the nation. What is needed is not the giving of vast amounts of resources - the needs can never be met - but the giving of ourselves that others might have hope and their lives in turn change.

CHAPTER ELEVEN

MISSIONS

Nobody should ever attempt to discuss anything regarding the Church without covering the issue of missions because it is the heartbeat of God. As the Church is the barometer of the nation so missions is the barometer of the Church. It amazes me that the moment a Church begins to experience financial problems, the first thing to be cut is the missions budget.

The Word, "missionary" is derived from the Greek, "Apostello" which means, "to send." From this, of course, we get the word Apostle. The same Latin word is "Mittio" - to send - or "missio" which is a "sending away." Jesus is *the* apostle or missionary par excellence. He was sent of the Father and the Spirit for the mission of redemption. A missionary then, is one sent out with authority to perform a special duty. A missionary does not speak on his own initiative but as a commissioned agent. Most importantly, missionaries are not born, they are made. Now, every Christian is bound to be a witness but not every witness is a missionary. Sadly today the witnesses are sent as missionaries and because they do not have the authority, they cannot perform the task.

In Matthew's Gospel we are given three specific commands of Christ in relationship to calling and ministry:

1. Come Matt 11:28 which appertains to **CONVERSION**
2. Follow Matt 16:24 which appertains to **DISCIPLESHIP**
3. Go Matt 9:38 which appertains to **MISSIONARY**

The four main facets of missionary life are given by Paul the Apostle in Romans 10:13-15:-

1. The One who **sends**
2. The one who is **sent**
3. Those **to whom** they are sent
4. The **message**

Nobody in the Book of Acts was ever sent or went without due process of **PRAYER** and **FASTING** (acts 13:2). The missionaries were specifically :
1. Separated for **HIM** personally
2. Under **HIS** authority and direction
3. Sent forth of the **Holy Ghost**

Oh indeed, they were sent out from a local church for, *"when they had fasted and prayed and layed their hands on them, they sent them away."* The setting out of missionaries from a local Church manifests three distinct acts of the Holy Spirit :
1. They were called to work **ABROAD.**
2. The call was made known **BY THE HOLY SPIRIT** when the Church was in a fit spiritual condition.
3. They were sent forth **BY THE HOLY GHOST**.

Today the church sends but also holds. How? Monetarily. Often those who are sent are absolutely rigidly controlled through the finances. This often leads to frustrations and then splits between missionaries and their home base. Alternatively, conditions are often imposed as to time, area of operation and such like which can constrict the workings of the Holy Spirit to get His programmes achieved.

John 4:35 declares, *"The fields are white already unto Harvest.... Pray ye therefore that the Lord........"* There are a total of 2,974 major languages on the face of the earth and to date slightly over 1,185 have been reached and have the Bible in their language. That's hardly believable in this modern age but absolutely true. It is the express responsibility of the Church not only to endeavour to reach **EVERY CREATURE** in this generation but to prepare the next generation to reach theirs. The Church is falling behind the programme of world-wide evangelism. Why? For the simple reason that we have not been doing the task God's way.

Though many may think that Africa is evangelised, there are vast reaches of this enormous Continent which have never been penetrated with the Gospel and, until the Church sends out her very best to perform the task, they never will be reached. How different the great missionary endeavour of the last century, when Britain sent forth from her shores the very best of her sons and daughters. The creme de la creme of her universities went to such inhospitable places as Burma, India, China, the Heart of Africa, the Islands. Today in our endeavour to build our personal *empire* we send forth the slop, the left-overs, the local church embarrassment to perform the highest, most honorary task of the local church: missions. I once had a missionary who came with such a powerful testimonial from the pastor that I believed I was receiving the incredible gem that every missionary dreams about. I soon discovered that the pastor was actually fully supporting the missionary to get rid of her as she had become such an embarrassment to the local church that it was worth the support money each month to be rid of that person. What a far cry from the Paul and Silas and Timothy to what is sent forth today.

There is not a single local church in South Africa that should not be endeavouring to send out a missionary - at least one - not to some other part of South Africa but to the remotest corner of this vast Continent. "That's impractical," you say. And that's why it doesn't happen because where there is no vision, the people perish. The royal argument is that there usually is not the finances to salary a pastor plus send out a missionary. Well, if the Church would get on its knees and fast and pray and stay fasting and praying until something broke, then the local Church would explode numerically and financially so that a missionary could be sent forth.

Until we really get the Holy Spirit agenda we will struggle and strive to no avail. Furthermore, I cannot believe the waste that goes on in the Kingdom. It is absolutely criminal how much money is poured into sewers when we are commanded to be wise stewards of God's heritage. We invest in buildings, vehicles and things instead of people who are eternal.

What I am saying, though true, may only inspire anger. But, if we really operated according to the heart beat of God, we would agonise and travail and wrestle until His Word was being fulfilled in our midst.

I have been in many areas of Africa where people have never heard of Jesus let alone seen a white man. I could take you to remote tribes in the Zambezi River basin who are so primitive that they do not even wear clothes or live in any kind of permanent dwellings. But this is 1996!

What will grip our hearts again and steer us back on the right course? What will enflame our vision so that the giant might arise and train up an army of its best soldiers to thrust them out on to a war-torn, weary Continent? What will inspire our imaginations so that we see the multitudes of our very Africa marching to a Christless eternity and realise that, not only do we have the answer, but we have also the power to do something about it. It is going to take prayer, prayer and more prayer until our whole beings are saturated with God and our very lives are to do His will.

Missions are not an option; they are an absolute command. Any single denomination could make a startling impact on Mocambique in this hour. Why is the Zionist cult making such inroads not only in South Africa but in Mocambique? Because they are expected, nay demanded to sacrifice and to go forth evangelising, while we sit comfortably on our pews. The Mormons - everyone - are required to devote two years of their lives to missions *before* embarking on anything else in life. The costs: met by their own families who are still required to tithe over and above their personal commitment to missions. Why is it so successful? Because it is an honour, a privilege, highly esteemed to send forth their best young men and women to reach "the lost."

South African Church, you need to grasp a vision of the *NEED*. Then there must be a looking to *HIM* and not to the impossibilities presented by a thousand difficulties and excuses. He alone is our resource, provision, strength and inspiration. The greatest missionary of the Modern Age, Hudson Taylor of China said, "God's work done in His way will never lack His provision." Resting only on the unchanging Word of an unchanging God, Hudson Taylor ventured forth to the wilds and hostility of China with no friends, no support, no mission board and no promises except *HIS*. He was called a "no good upstart," "a trouble maker," "rebellious" and every other epithet which could be imagined. Scorn and ridicule was poured out upon the young missionary who was enflamed with the fire of God.

Missions must be re-instituted with the calling, dignity and honour which God intended. Only then will the Church attain her highest purpose once again. Awake South Africa. It is one thing to take your place in the brotherhood of nations but what about your place in the roll call of God? It is long overdue time that we stopped debating theology and argued and strived over nonessential differences which have been blown into divisions. It is time to raise up the standard and banner of God and march to His drumbeat.

"All of Africa shall be saved
By the Gospel of Jesus ...."

so the little chorus goes. It will never happen unless the Church is prepared to do something. The great Gospel evangelist has his place but he can never substitute for the missionary apostle who sets forth to plant and establish solid work.

CHAPTER TWELVE

TRANSITION

Despite the euphoria about a New South Africa, the nation is still in transition and it is the next three years which will tell in what direction the die will irrevocably be cast.

It is pretty sad and disgusting that South Africa has declared herself to no longer be a Christian nation. I should like to see any Middle Eastern country tolerate Christianity let alone declare themselves to be non-Islamic. Actually, it is forbidden by flogging and even death to hold any kind of spiritual gathering in Saudi Arabia other than Islamic even in the privacy of one's own home. Furthermore, Christians and Jews are totally forbidden entrance to the religious sites of Mecca and Medina. What a tragedy that the "Christian West" is bending over backwards to accommodate and give full rights to every "ism" and religion that desires to take advantage of the liberality. Even in Israel, by law of the Supreme Court, a Jew who receives Christ and converts to Christianity loses his Israeli nationality!

Despite apartheid and the sinful corruption of men, South Africa was founded upon Christian principles and it is upon these principles the nation must stand. Any other system brings the worst excesses of barbarity or a total decline of morals and ethics. Look at the inhumanity of nations suffering under a medieval-type system of Islamic Law. Nobody shouts about the violation of human rights in Kuwait, Saudi Arabia, Syria, Iran and an almost endless list of others.

The Church in South Africa has three short years to force change, demand change and execute change to bring South Africa back to being a Christian nation. "Impossible," you say, "but with Him nothing is impossible." Every Church throughout South Africa must dispense with their regular meetings and programmes and begin to call special prayer services which will resound around the nation and shake her to her very foundations bringing the terrifying fear of God back into operation. What a mandate but what awful consequences for failure. The price is high, the stakes even higher.

Unless the Church of South Africa mobilises, fully mobilises, her very resources right now, it will soon be too late and the only result will be ICHABOD. Everybody will suffer as a consequence.

Church of the Lord Jesus Christ, you and you alone are the answer to the violence, the anger, the hatred. You alone are the answer to the immorality and corruption. You alone know and must practise the only TRUE standard: the Word of the Lord. Without such, the consequences are too terrible to contemplate. Church, you alone must stand against the "equal rights" of witchcraft which brings darkness and fear and enslaves people in a system far worse than apartheid.

I have no doubt that the Hand of God is holding South Africa in check at this time, so giving her a chance to rise up to her High Calling. No man, let me repeat, no man is responsible for the peace in South Africa. If there is any part played by any, all glory must go to Him, Prince of Peace and King of Kings who saw fit to use a frail vessel such as man for His purposes and designs. The Word is clear. *"Let no man think more highly of himself than he ought."* Indeed of ourselves we are nothing and He is everything. Not only does the future of South Africa depend upon the Church in South Africa but the future of the Church in Africa also depends upon you. That is an heavily awesome responsibility. Some will say, "We don't want it; we didn't ask for it." My answer is, "too bad! God has given it to you, so rise up and do something about it."

There is a judgement of the nations, living nations at the Second Coming of Jesus. This judgement will be basically according to the treatment of Israel and Jesus Himself will divide the nations into "sheep" nations and "goat" nations. Jesus said, *"My sheep hear My voice and I know them, and they follow Me...."* (Jn 10:27). Goats are full of rebellion and "But... but.... but.....!" While in the old days sheep and goats were permitted to graze together during the day, they were kept separated at night because the goats would cause a stampede, get up to mischief and lead the sheep astray. So then, Jesus in likening nations to sheep and goats is obviously referring to those who are obedient and those who are not. This is further enforced in the Book of Revelation.

It is quite conceivable that under the current dispensation of ANC Government, South Africa will no longer support Israel. Unless there is a major Christian backlash right now, South Africa is in imminent danger of degenerating into the moral and ethical chaos which currently plagues the west. Firstly, there must be a will to do something and this will must then be put into concerted action through absolute consensus. From where will consensus come? Prayer, prayer and more prayer. There needs to be strong heart-wrenching cries and sobs until we allow the Holy Spirit to break through the emotions and soul realm of our lives and get down to the nitty-gritty motives which direct us. When it is no longer an issue of "who's right," or "what do I want" but, "Lord what is really Your will?" only then will progress be made. God is not going to tell one person one thing and another person something different. What stands in the way of the same message coming through is the "I" factor which is only dealt with by persevering prayer.

In the vision of Chapter Two, South Africa was portrayed as the loins and legs of a marathon runner who had dropped from the race because of muscle cramp and fatigue. What is so important now is that the Church, the whole Church in South Africa does not settle down into that "Kay Serah" mentality and just let things happen. It is now a proven fact that since prayer was taken out of the schools in America in 1962 there has been a consistent decline in educational standards let alone morals and ethics. Morality deals with man's relationship to God while ethics deals with man's relationship to man. The absence of Biblical principles such as the death sentence, corporal punishment and prayer puts men at odds with God because of disobedience and rebellion. If men are at odds with God, they will most certainly be at odds with one another, hence the increase of armed violence, lawlessness and rebellion in the society. If South Africa cannot sort out its own evils it can never be used to address the problems of the Continent at large. Of course the sceptics would ask if there is, indeed, a moral and ethical obligation to do something in the Continent. I have no doubt that God ordained such for South Africa and not to rise to the call of Africa and the occasion places South Africa in a "goat" role. Jesus declares, *"Come inherit the Kingdom.... for I was an hungered and ye gave me meat: I was thirsty, and ye gave me drink: I was a stranger and ye took me in: naked and ye clothed me: I was sick and ye visited me: I was in prison and ye came unto me. Then shall the righteous answer him saying Lord when....? And the King shall answer and say unto them, verily I say unto you, inasmuch as ye have done it unto **one of the least of these my brethren**, ye have done it unto me."*

This is in no wise giving precedence or legitimacy to any kind of social gospel.

What an enormously honourable task God has offered to the Church in South Africa. Will the denominational leaders not join together, lay aside their differences and rise up to the occasion and High Calling of Almighty God? There is no other answer, no other alternative. It is a question of marching to the drum beat of heaven and the trumpet call of God or degenerate into luke warmness and mediocrity. I remember many years ago standing on the ramparts of the great castle in Belfast. I looked out across a war-torn city and war-torn Northern Ireland with its fears, hatreds and religious and political divisions. As I stood there the Lord began to unravel a scroll containing the entire blue-print for reconciliation and peace in all of Ireland. Well, who was I except a simple African preacher. Miraculously, God brought me into a meeting of spiritual leaders in Belfast. They rejected the message because they rejected the messenger. Peace could have and would have come to Northern Ireland over twelve years ago: a lasting peace because what God does He does well. Today the fruit of that rejection is still evident in the hatred, the violence, the bombings and endless debates between Dublin, Belfast and Whitehall. Still the crisis is not solved. God had given the Church - the true Church - the unique opportunity to arise above their petty politics, narrow minded interpretations, jealousies and differences to be a light and standard in the darkness and chaos. That they did not even attempt to join together and rise to the occasion reveals just how narrow God's people were. And so the tragedy goes on.

Will you, South Africa take the same stance? Will the church fail to call national days of prayer and fasting? Can stadiums throughout South Africa not hold masses of united Christians with one aim in mind - to lift up the name of Jesus and declare Him to be Lord over South Africa? Can the mass army of the Lord Jesus for once march under His banner and standard to demand a Christian South Africa instead of a denomination, a Church or a personal slogan?

Not only is South Africa awaiting the giant to rise, but all of Africa is waiting. Church, will you one more time shake yourself out of your lethargy, out of your complacency, out of your isolationism and be the glorious, triumphant Church of which the Word speaks. All of creation is groaning and travailing for the manifested sons. Who are they? Those who so dwell in Christ that it is the glory. And, when the lion roars, the world will take note.

A VISION FOR AFRICA

Shekinah/Kalibu Ministries is still operating in Southern and Central Africa. Their main base is in Blantyre, Malawi where one of their present projects is to build an elite, private secondary school which will cater for the future leaders of Malawi both in the business and political arena. Not only will the students receive an excellent education but they will also receive grounding in the Word of God. The school in Malawi has just had the foundations poured as of July 96. This is a pilot scheme and should it prove successful for Malawi we plan to build similar schools in Mocambique, Zambia and Tanzania.

If you would like to contribute towards this project we would appreciate any donations. The total cost of a school is U.S. $300,000. We are registered in the United States of America as a non profit corporation under Shekinah Ministries so all donations will be tax deductible.

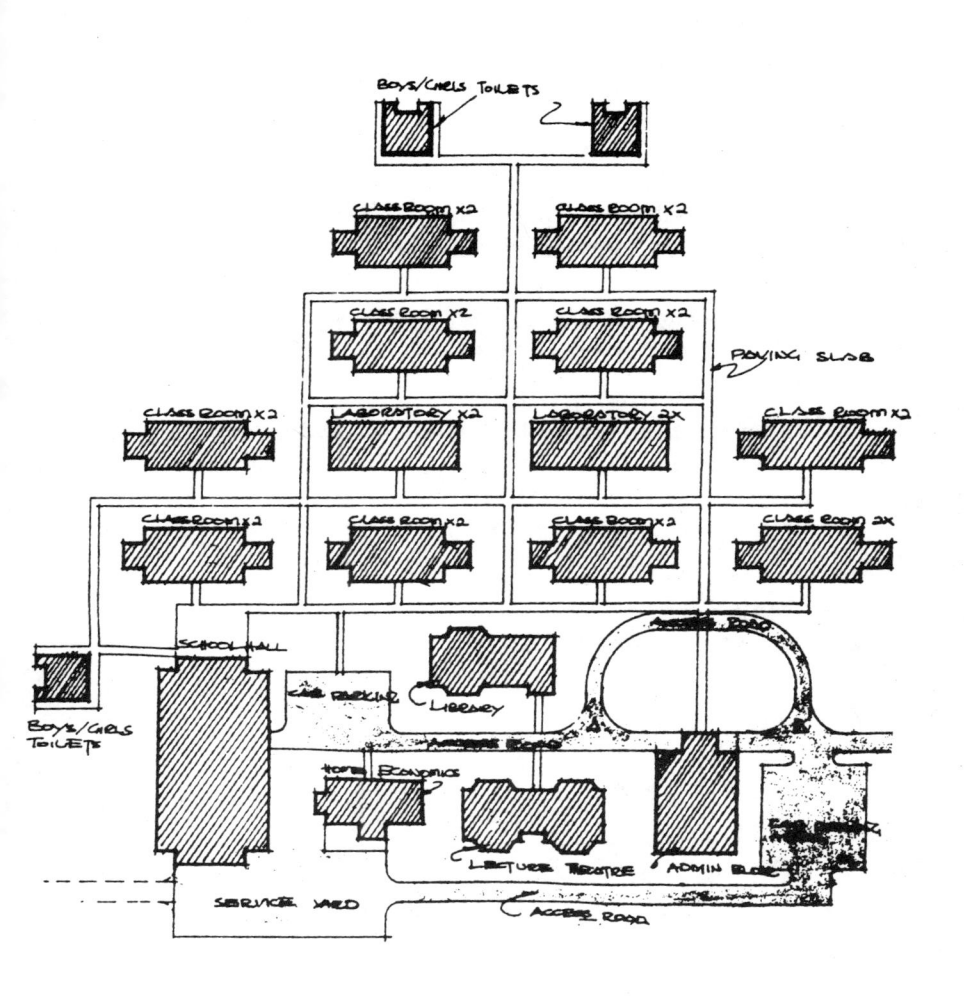

PLAN OF BUILDINGS FOR SECONDARY SCHOOL

Other books by the same author:-
RECKLESSLY ABANDONED
LOVE CONSTRAINED
Both powerful testimonies of life and ministry during the Rhodesian bush war and the civil war in Mocambique.
THE ONLY GOOD ONE'S A DEAD ONE
A study on the characteristics of African snakes with a comparison to the devil.
TALES OF A MODERN DAY INTERCESSOR
THE PRICE OF DISOBEDIENCE

For further information regarding the work of this ministry or should you desire to support Shekinah/Kalibu Ministries please contact us at any of the following:-

SHEKINAH MINISTRIES
P.O. Box 34685
Kansas City, MO 64116, U.S.A.
Tel. (816) 452-5315
Fax (816) 452-5457

KALIBU MINISTRIES
P.O. Box 1473
Blantyre, Malawi, Central Africa
Tel 011-265-633187